8

THE DAYSTAR VOYAGES

THE FROZEN SPACE PILOT

GILBERT MORRIS
AND DAN MEEKS

MOODY PRESS
CHICAGO

©1999 by
GILBERT MORRIS
AND
DANIEL MEEKS

All rights reserved. No part of this book may be reproduced in any form without permission in writing from the publisher, except in the case of brief quotations embodied in critical articles or reviews.

All Scripture quotations, unless indicated, are taken from the *New American Standard Bible*, © 1960, 1962, 1963, 1968, 1971, 1972, 1973, 1975, 1977, and 1994 by The Lockman Foundation, La Habra, Calif. Used by permission.

ISBN: 0-8024-4112-2

1 3 5 7 9 10 8 6 4 2

Printed in the United States of America

To my sister, Rose Sparkman

Cissi, I've thought about you many times over the years. What I remember most is your humor and quick wit. Because you are a truly generous and caring person, you are a delight to be around. Too bad we've lived apart so many years. I love you.

Danny

Characters

The *Daystar* ....an intergalactic star cruiser

The *Daystar* Space Rangers:
- Jerusha Ericson, 15....a topflight engineer
- Raina St. Clair, 14.......the ship's communications officer
- Mei-Lani Lao, 13 ....*Daystar*'s historian and linguist
- Ringo Smith, 14...........a computer wizard
- Heck Jordan, 15..........an electronics genius
- Dai Bando, 16..............known for his exceptional physical abilities

The *Daystar* Officers:
- Mark Edge ....*Daystar*'s young captain
- Zeno Thrax..................the first officer
- Bronwen Llewellen ....the navigator; Dai's aunt
- Ivan Petroski...............the chief engineer
- Temple Cole ....the flight surgeon
- Tara Jaleel ....the weapons officer
- Studs Cagney ....the crew chief

Contents

1
A Gift for Jaleel

"I'm a genius! There's no other way to look at it. I'm just a genius, and there's no doubt about it!"

Ringo Smith glanced up at his friend Heck Jordan, who was busy admiring himself in the mirror.

Ringo was a thin fourteen-year-old himself, with brown hair and hazel eyes. As he studied Heck, he absently fingered the medallion that dangled from a gold chain around his neck. It had an image of Sir Richard Irons on one side. Richard Irons was known as the worst pirate in the galaxy. And when Ringo Smith had learned that Irons was his father, he had been tempted to throw the medallion away.

Now he leaned back against the bulkhead of the *Daystar* and couldn't help smiling. "You just come right out and admit that, do you, Heck? That you're a genius?"

"I'd like to deny it, but I always tell the truth."

Heck Jordan drew a candy bar from his pocket, ripped off the paper, and took half of it in one tremendous bite. Then he flipped the paper onto the dusty floor. "You just don't know how lucky you are to be around me, Ringo. One of these days you'll be saying, 'I knew Heck Jordan when he was just a boy—before his outstanding inventions made him the richest man in the galaxy.'"

Ringo well knew that Heck was in fact an electronics genius. He was also very overweight, and he loved loud clothing. Even now he wore a purple neckerchief that clashed with his official uniform.

The *Daystar* Space Rangers—which both boys were —all thought they had handsome uniforms. Each wore the standard slate gray tunic with silver trim on the collar and sleeves. Each ranger also wore navy pants with a silver stripe down each side. Black half boots with synthetic rubber soles completed the uniforms.

At the moment, the boys stood in the passageway outside the training room, ready as far as possible for their Jai-Kando martial arts practice.

Their fussy instructor demanded that students arrive at each training session outfitted in their white martial arts outfits. But today there had been no time to change clothes before arriving for the training period. Today was different because they had just finished repairing the long-range scanners. Actually, it had been Heck who solved the glitch in the servo matrix.

Their instructor was Weapons Officer Tara Jaleel, and Ringo dreaded the lieutenant as much as he dreaded a case of Tenorian Mung. Tenorian Mung was the heavyweight champion of skin diseases in the galaxy. No one in his right mind would want his body covered with large, painful purple-and-blue welts. Tara Jaleel, on the other hand, was a grand master of Jai-Kando. Either Jaleel or Tenorian Mung could make a ranger's life extremely miserable.

Perhaps it was this dread of what was to come that made Ringo reluctant to argue with Heck. Ringo just stood waiting, heart thumping, and his hands locked behind him.

Although the *Daystar* was passing through space at an enormous rate of speed, there was little or no sensation of movement. Through the port across from where he stood, Ringo could see the blackness of space. A glorious display of stars seemed to stretch on forever. It made a beautiful sight, and he knew that he was seeing only a small part of the billions and trillions of lights that God had set in the heavens.

"I think I'm getting sick," Heck said suddenly. He popped the other half of the candy bar in his mouth and then looked apprehensively down the hall. "Let's go let Dr. Cole take a look at me. I may be coming down with some strange unheard-of disease." He held out one arm and pulled up his sleeve. "Doesn't that look like a welt to you?"

Ringo grinned suddenly in spite of himself. "I think I know what your strange, unheard-of disease is. It's called Tara Jaleel-itis."

"I'm not afraid of Lieutenant Jaleel!"

"No, you're not afraid of her. You're terrified of her. Just like everybody else." Ringo looked knowingly straight into Heck's eyes.

Heck Jordan stared back resentfully. "I'm not afraid of her," he repeated defiantly. He kicked dust on Ringo's boots. Then he leaned over and squinted at the floor. "Hmm," he pondered. "I wonder where all this dust came from?"

Ringo looked, too. The corridor floor was indeed covered with a thin layer of ash gray dust—something most unusual in a spacecraft.

But he ignored Heck's comment, looked up at the ceiling, and shivered. "Well, she scares *me* to death! And if you're not afraid of her, you're about the only one of us rangers who isn't—except for Dai Bando."

"You know what I think?" Heck said. "Sometimes I think she's not even a woman. I think she's a man in disguise."

"It sure seems that way sometimes. A couple of days ago, Mei-Lani was reading up on the tribes that were in the lieutenant's family tree. They were Masai warriors back on Earth in the old days. They were so fierce that nobody could stand against them, and the women were just as brave and warlike as the men."

Thoughtfully, Ringo started tracing lines in the dust with the toe of his boot. "The history banks say that some of the female Masai warriors had no fear at all and could easily kill ten men in no time. And they worshiped that goddess Shiva."

"I know. Like the little statue you carry around in your pocket," Heck interrupted. "Why don't you just get rid of that thing?"

But Ringo just went on talking. "Their enemies called the female Masai warriors 'Shiva's Arms.' They said their arms moved so fast when they handled weapons that you couldn't see them." He paused. "At least, that's what Mei-Lani told me."

"I heard that Mei-Lani's been in sick bay."

"Yes, she has. I visit her every day. But you have to visit her through the quarantine shield."

Apparently it had never occurred to Heck Jordan to visit Mei-Lani Lao. "What's wrong with her?" He started on another candy bar.

"Dr. Cole hasn't figured it out yet. She thinks it's a virus, but she's still running tests."

"Maybe I'll stop by for a visit and cheer her up with my genius self."

"Remember, she's in quarantine, so you aren't going to get in. And I know Dr. Cole wouldn't want Mei-Lani to catch some of your gigantic ego."

Heck looked ready to argue that he would certainly get in if he wanted to, but at that moment Lieutenant Tara Jaleel stepped through the door at the end of the corridor. Both of the Space Rangers straightened up, and Ringo felt a flicker of fear go down his spine.

Tara Jaleel walked purposefully down the passageway toward them. The weapons officer of the

Daystar was a fierce looking woman indeed, though she was rather attractive. Fully six feet tall, she had flashing eyes and the sculptured features of the old Masai. Her skin had a glistening quality about it. She was carrying a medium-sized cargo container along with a Dyno-Vac. Ringo knew that both were heavy, but she carried them with ease. Jaleel was a strong woman.

"Good morning, Lieutenant," Heck said quickly. "I hope you're feeling well today."

Tara Jaleel glared at the two of them. If looks could have killed, Ringo was sure they would have died instantly.

She marched past them into the training room and—when Ringo and Heck were about to follow—said abruptly, "There will be no training sessions for a few days."

Both Ringo and Heck stood staring. Tara Jaleel *never* canceled a training session! Finally Ringo cleared his throat and found his voice. "Do I understand you correctly, Lieutenant? There will be no training sessions."

"No. Not until I give further orders. You are dismissed."

Ringo could see that the training room deck was covered with fine debris and ashes. The lieutenant set down the Dyno-Vac and the container and began vacuuming. The resulting dust cloud was so heavy that it drifted out into the corridor. Then, suddenly, Tara Jaleel turned off the Dyno-Vac and stood stock-still, looking off into space. Her eyes seemed to glaze over.

Ringo did not know what they should do. He couldn't read Tara's mind, but he sensed that some major occurrence had taken place—something that the lieutenant did not intend to talk about.

In any event, it was difficult to believe that Tara

Jaleel would forgo the pleasure of pummeling them until they were black and blue. That seemed to give her pleasure, and the Jai-Kando sessions were always a torment.

Heck whispered, “What do we do, Ringo?”

“You go on back. I’ve got to talk to the lieutenant a minute.”

“Talk to her! About what?”

“It’s a—a private business,” Ringo answered.

“OK, but I think you’re crazy. I just hope we never have another one of those awful Jai-Kando sessions again.” He turned and started up the passageway, leaving Ringo alone at the door with Tara Jaleel.

He waited nervously. In truth, he was afraid of the weapons officer at any time, whether or not they were in a training session. As he hesitated, he wished he had never gotten himself entangled with Jai-Kando and with Jaleel’s goddess, Shiva, in the first place.

He was about to run after Heck, but then Raina St. Clair’s face flashed into his mind. She was unsmiling, and her stern look seemed to keep him focused on the task at hand.

Ringo was very attracted to Raina St. Clair, the communications expert. To Ringo she was the prettiest girl in the world. Raina had not seemed particularly interested in him, however. She seemed to like another member of the crew, Dai Bando.

Still, Ringo very much wanted her approval. And Tara Jaleel had assured Ringo that her goddess had the power he needed to attract Raina’s attention. So, though Ringo was a Christian and should have known better, he bought a tiny statue of Shiva and carried it in his pocket. The thing seemed to have some sort of power all right, but it was not a power that Ringo found pleasant. He had been plagued with nothing but feelings of doubt and despair ever since.

As he stood waiting for courage to speak to Tara Jaleel, he couldn't help noticing that her giant statue of the goddess was no longer there.

Finally she seemed to come out of her trancelike daze and to see him for the first time. "What is it you want, Smith?"

"Well, Lieutenant, I—I'm just wondering what happened here. This—over there is where that huge statue of Shiva stood . . ."

Tara Jaleel hesitated. Then she said, "I was trying to move the statue, and it toppled over on the deck and broke."

Instantly Ringo knew that she was lying. There was a shifty look in her eyes. Besides, a fallen statue could not have created such tiny fragments as he saw lying on the deck. Grainy gray dust was everywhere. But he could not imagine what could have happened.

"Well, that's too bad," he said. He tried to pull his thoughts together, then reached into his pocket and drew out the small statue of Shiva. "I wanted to give you this, Lieutenant. Even before I knew what had happened."

"Keep it. You need it."

"Well, actually I don't think I want to. If you don't mind, I'd rather you take it."

Ringo saw anger flash in her eyes. But then she gave him a forced smile. "We'll talk about this later," she said, taking the statue from his hand.

"Sure, Lieutenant, that will be fine."

Ringo turned and left the training room, feeling definitely confused. He found Heck waiting for him down the corridor. "You didn't have to wait," he said.

"I wanted to find out what happened. You're not trying to get in thick with that woman, are you?"

"No. Not at all."

"What did you want to talk to her about?"

"Heck, you've got more curiosity than a cat."

Heck spread his hands apart and said plaintively, "Why, Ringo, old buddy. After all, we're friends."

Ringo was always uncomfortable when Heck called him "buddy." Heck Jordan was a con artist. His schemes were innumerable, and Ringo had learned that anyone caught up in them inevitably came to be in deep trouble.

"Every time you call me 'buddy,' Heck, I know you want something."

"You're too suspicious, Ringo. I just want to be your friend—give you my help. Most people would be grateful to have a friend like me."

Ringo shot a suspicious glance at Heck. At the same time he sensed how much better he felt now that the statue of Shiva was gone from his pocket. He had not understood how much it had affected him. *It's like a load's been lifted off my back*, he thought.

Other *Daystar* Space Rangers had talked to him about the dangers of getting involved with the world of evil spirits. But he had been so eager to win Raina's approval that he had blocked out their warnings. Now he felt so lighthearted that he began to whistle a tune, slightly off-key, as he used to do.

"Hey, Ringo," Heck said, as they strode along the long main corridor that went the length of the star cruiser, "I've been thinking about something."

"I'm against it," Ringo said.

"You haven't even heard what it is yet."

"I don't have to know what it is. The last time I helped you, we almost got ourselves thrown off this ship."

"That wasn't my fault," Heck protested loudly.

"Not your fault!" Ringo retorted hotly. "That's just

the problem with you, Heck. Nothing is ever your fault. You blame everybody and everything except yourself for your mess ups! You're a victim of your own self. You should learn to control these wild impulses you have."

"I didn't mess up. Think about it." Heck lowered his voice. "You and me, ol' buddy, we created a holographic virtual reality machine that worked. No one's ever done that before. I can't help it if Captain Edge doesn't recognize genius when he sees it."

"Heck, being on this ship means everything to me. I'm not going to let you talk me into another one of your harebrained schemes." He crossed his arms over his chest. "Whatever you do, leave me out of it."

Heck waved a hand in the air. "Don't you worry about that, buddy. That's all over. I just want to bounce another idea off of you."

"So what have you got on your mind now?" Ringo grumbled.

"Well, I'm going to get into the security computer's memory storage banks."

Ringo looked blankly at him. This was the computer that recorded all of the *Daystar*'s activities. "You'll get thrown off the ship for sure. You know what Captain Edge said. He'd get rid of both of us if we tried any more schemes. And you promised you wouldn't."

Heck laughed loudly. "But I had my fingers crossed."

"A lie is a lie no matter how many fingers you have crossed."

Heck just shrugged his shoulders and grinned.

Ringo sighed. He knew Heck never worried about trouble until he was neck deep in it.

"A man's got to do what a man's got to do," Heck said, and he laughed again.

Heck Jordan said no more about his plan. But as

he walked along beside Ringo, he thought again of how he could steal the data chips and show a video of Jaleel and the collapsing statue at some Space Ranger party.

Heck's overactive mind screamed vengeance. He thought, *Boy, that'll get her for all the times she's beaten me black and blue. Just one look at her face when that statue fell over—smashing to ashes—that'll hurt her worse than anything!*

Tara Jaleel worked slowly, cautiously, even tenderly, as she vacuumed the floor with the Dyno-Vac. This particular statue of Shiva had been crafted thousands of years ago by the Denebians. Each dust particle, each dirt fragment, each gray flake of ash was precious to her. The Dyno-Vac was especially suited for this work. It could suck cobwebs out of a mortar joint at a hundred feet. The machine worked quietly as it funneled Shiva's remains into the cargo container.

Reaching the corridor, the Masai warrior saw the place where Heck's big foot had made tracks in Shiva's remains. The thought of those two boys walking in Shiva's dust—walking on the goddess herself!—infuriated her.

Her eyes reflected the rage that burned red hot in her soul. She thought, *One day, whoever destroyed Shiva will pay dearly. If it takes my whole life, I will avenge her for this deed.*

Tara Jaleel stood straight and tall. She raised her arms toward the ceiling in defiance. "*Ai-yee-aa.*" The Masai wailing cry filled the air of the training room four times in a row.

Then the lieutenant started performing the Jai-Kando warm-up routines. Her skin glistened more than usual as arms and legs moved faster and faster. They moved almost too fast for the eye to follow.

A voice spoke to her mind then, and Tara Jaleel braced herself. She knew that the one who spoke to her would punish the failures of her followers.

Failure was the last consideration of Tara Jaleel.

2

Heck Gets a Mentor

Capt. Mark Edge looked much like an ancient Viking. He had blond hair, light blue-gray eyes, and—at six one and one hundred ninety pounds—he was in perfect shape. Although he had once been close to being a space pirate, he was happily walking a straight line under the direction of Galactic Command leadership. He was a capable captain.

Just now, Captain Edge was upset. His lips were drawn together in a grim line as he studied the officers that he had called to Engineering for this special meeting. There was the chief engineer—Petroski—a dwarf who had an iron will of giant proportions. Edge knew he was one of the best engineers in the Space Federation. Studs Cagney, the crew chief, stood waiting for the captain to make his announcement. Cagney had been a rough man indeed. But since the young Space Rangers had come on board, he had been listening to their talk about Jesus. Though Cagney had the same thinning black hair and short, muscular frame as always, the captain had to admit that his crew chief had a better attitude than he once had.

The third member of the team was the most unusual in appearance. This was Zeno Thrax, the first officer. A perfect albino with white hair and colorless eyes, rather chilling to look at, Thrax came from Mentor Seven. There was nothing on that planet but mines. All the people lived underground, and all were albinos. For some reason, Zeno had been driven from his home and could never return.

Edge said, "I expect that you're wondering why I've called you all together. Well, to be brief, it's about Heck Jordan."

"Not him again!" Petroski groaned.

"What's he done now?" Cagney growled.

"He hasn't really *done* anything since he broke into the main power cells on our last trip."

"I think you should have thrown him off the ship for that," Petroski groused. "And all the rest of these Space Rangers at the same time. It's like running a nursery in space."

Captain Edge knew good and well that Petroski actually was rather fond of all the Space Rangers—except for Heck, who drove him crazy.

"Get rid of Jordan is what I say! We haven't got time to baby-sit him."

"Well," Edge said, "that was pretty much my thought at first. But the truth is—I know he's as pesky as a chigger, but he's also about the best electronics man I've ever run across."

"I agree with you," the first officer said. Zeno Thrax's face usually showed little emotion, but his pale eyes did gleam now. "As a matter of fact, I rather like Heck."

"Like him!" Petroski groaned again. "How can you like him? He keeps things stirred up all the time, and I like things to go nice and even."

"Well, geniuses are like that," Thrax said calmly. "They have all this energy, and they can't channel it."

Studs Cagney frowned at the first officer. "And you really think Jordan's a *genius?*"

"Yes, I do. I think the boy is a genius."

Edge was interested in Zeno's opinion. "I know he's smart and all that, but—"

"It's more than that, Captain." Thrax was obviously trying to put his thoughts in order, as he always did before speaking. He was a very methodical man. "Those with just ordinary abilities can do all that can be done in a normal way. But once in a while someone comes along who breaks all the rules. They think in a different way. They get insights that the rest of us don't have. Look at Beethoven, for example—that great musician from long ago. He was writing symphonies when he was six years old. Some men spend sixty years at it and never write a good one. But he did it when he was a mere child."

The three officers discussed Heck Jordan back and forth, and Edge stood quietly listening. It was hard being captain of a spaceship, for even one's smallest decisions could easily mean life or death. Finally he broke in on the discussion, saying, "I agree with you, Ivan, that Jordan is a pain oftentimes. But he did do some good work on our last voyage. And his virtual reality invention did save the life of Captain Murphy when we lost the *Wellington*."

"And I'd have to agree to that," Studs Cagney said. "So what are you going to do with him, Captain?"

"I think we've got to find a way to channel his energies. He needs the adults in this crew to help him with discipline. Jaleel has been trying with the physical training, and it's not working. But somehow we'll have to train him. If we don't, he'll wind up stripping out every circuit on the ship for his pet projects."

"He's very self-serving." Zeno nodded. "Very self-serving. But geniuses are often like that."

"Well," Edge said, "I want a program set in place that will keep him busy. I want a volunteer to mentor him."

"What does that mean—to 'mentor him'?" Studs Cagney asked, frowning.

"It means to be responsible for him. To be sure he doesn't get in trouble—take a real interest in him as a person."

"Well, *I* can't do it, Captain," Cagney said. "We just don't get along, Jordan and me."

"I don't think I can do it either, Captain." That was Zeno. "As I said, I like Heck well enough, but I'm not electronically qualified to understand his work."

Edge turned to Ivan Petroski and grinned. "Looks like it's up to you, Ivan. You must have done something good to get a reward like this."

Ivan Petroski stiffened. He stared wildly at the captain. He stared at the other two officers. He began waving his arms in the air. "Not me! I can't do it! I can't baby-sit this crew!"

Captain Edge allowed him to protest for a while. Then he said, "I'm sorry, Ivan, but you're the only one who can handle this particular assignment. Do the best you can with him."

Petroski groaned. "All right. All right. I'll try, but I may wind up killing him."

After the other officers had left, Edge turned to Zeno Thrax and grinned. "I don't know who to feel sorry for, First," he said. "Heck or Ivan."

Most of the officers and crew on board the *Daystar* would never be considered famous. Bronwen Llewellen, however, *was* famous. At least she was famous among those who were familiar with the history of space exploration. She had achieved a reputation that far exceeded that of any other navigator. She had been a space pioneer and had flown on some of the first flights into deep space. Now, at the age of fifty-two, she was still fit and capable. Some said she had "second sight." She always denied that, but others were convinced that she had deeper insight into things than most people. And she was such a firm Christian that many of the crew came to her constantly for advice. Raina St. Clair especially enjoyed working with her.

"I don't think I'll ever learn all of this!" Raina wailed. She had joined Bronwen today to learn about maintenance of the new navigations and communications system. "Every time I come in here, Heck Jordan has changed things."

The nav and com systems were located down the corridor from the bridge. Heck had linked navigations, communications, and long-range scanners into a "cascading interlinked support matrix." This was Heck's fancy way of saying that these systems supported one another. If circuitry in navigations failed, similar circuitry in either communications or long-range scanners took over for the broken circuits.

As usual, Raina was wearing the uniform of the Space Rangers. She had auburn hair and an oval face and a dimple in her chin. Now she fixed her green eyes on the famous navigator and cried, "I just don't see how you get all this in your head, Bronwen! It has to be born in you, I think."

"Some of it does," the older woman agreed. She leaned back in her soft Dernof leather chair and smiled as though she was very fond of Raina. "Fortunately," she said, "most maintenance work doesn't require a great deal of thought."

"Well, I think this equipment's as hard to understand as—"

She broke off abruptly and knew she was blushing.

"As boys?" Bronwen offered gently.

Raina's cheeks felt warm. "How did you know I was thinking that? You do have second sight!"

Bronwen laughed a tinkling sound. "It doesn't take

second sight to know that young men and young women of your age are interested in each other. It's a very natural thing. I was the same when I was your age."

"Were you really, Bronwen?"

"Of course. I wasn't always an ancient wreck."

"You're not an ancient wreck!" Raina leaned forward, and her eyes grew thoughtful. "I thought at one time I understood boys, Bronwen, but now I don't think I ever will."

"And why do you think that?"

"Well, the ones that I like don't like me. And the ones that don't like me . . . well . . . I like *them*."

"Men are always trying to figure women out, Raina, and women are always trying to figure out men. That is likely to be a problem you'll have all of your life."

"But they never do? Figure out each other, I mean?"

"Sometimes they do. But men and women are so different. Boys and girls are different."

"How different, Bronwen?"

"Well, for example, when something important happens and someone asks a man what happened, he gives them a headline."

"What do you mean a headline?"

"Like on the old newspapers. A big headline like 'Mine Cave-in Kills Twenty People.' That's the way a man talks. He just gives the headline and thinks that's enough."

Raina saw the point and laughed out loud. "And women definitely aren't like that."

"No. We like to know the fine print. What happened? And where? And how? And what did it sound like? What did it feel like? That's why my husband and I sometimes got into arguments. He would come back from a long trip, and I'd say, 'What happened?'" She smiled fondly then and shook her head. "And he'd tell me in about ten words."

"So what would you do?"

"I'd push him into a chair and sit on his lap and grab his ears and say, 'You tell me every detail, or I'll pull your ears off.'"

Raina giggled with delight. She loved Bronwen Llewellen with all of her heart and had absorbed a great deal of wisdom from her.

The navigator continued talking while she adjusted a few dials. "But the universe is not a matter of male *versus* female."

"What do you mean?"

"The universe is filled with individuals who happen to *be* female and male. Both genders were created by the same God. God created them with differences—He obviously wanted them different, so He made them that way. But what a lot of people forget is that both genders think that the same values are important and worth developing."

"I can understand that."

"Of course, you can. In God's eyes there are differences in design and function, but as far as character and behavior are concerned, men and women have most things in common."

Raina did not talk for a while. She sat at the keyboard in front of the bank of instruments and thought. Something was on her mind. Abruptly she said, "I understand some of that. But you know how I feel about Dai Bando."

"I could hardly help knowing. Your eyes show that you feel very strongly about my nephew."

"Every time I look at Dai, my heart does a back flip."

Dai's aunt laughed. "That's very romantic, but you

might say the same thing about seeing a Cyronian lizard at your feet. Your heart would do a back flip then, too."

"That's not quite the same thing!"

"It's not far from it, though. Think of most love stories people read. They make falling in love sound a lot like catching a Trilox-IV flu virus."

"You mean falling in love is bad?"

"No, I mean that when someone falls in love in those stories, it says their heart beats faster, they begin to perspire, they breathe harder, their knees feel weak. Isn't that true?"

"Well, yes—"

"And that's what you feel when you have the flu, isn't it? Those are all physiological feelings."

"But didn't you feel any of those things when you met your future husband?"

Bronwen closed her eyes and thought awhile. "It's been so long ago, child. It's really hard to remember my first reactions. I do remember one thing, though, about our early days. I respected him more than any other human being I ever met. And I'd rather feel respect than experience all the heart back flips in the world." Then she said, "Once, when I was about your age, I did meet a boy that my heart did back flips over, but it came to nothing."

"But why not?"

"Because I finally decided that God had given him a different destiny from mine. We just weren't meant by God to be one." Then she said thoughtfully, "The same thing may be true for you and Dai. God has a plan for each one of us. He has one for you and one for Dai. And they may not flow together—although, of course, they may."

Raina thought she understood. She said, "Tell me more about the last boy."

But Bronwen Llewellen smiled and shook her head. "No. That's ancient history. Right now you've got to learn how to do these configurations with the console."

At that moment, the long-range scanners began chiming.

"Look, Bronwen! There's a ship!"

Bronwen leaned toward the screen. "Yes, I see it."

Raina's eyes narrowed. "It's a very small one, isn't it?"

"It's unbelievably small—and if it weren't for Heck's sensor improvements, it probably would never have been picked up by the scanners at all." Bronwen made some adjustments on the controls. "Maybe it's an escape pod. It appears to be about the right size for that." She watched the screen, then said, "It's drifting near the Lyra Sector. See?"

The navigator brought the Lyra Sector onto the console screen. "There's the Ring Nebula." She pointed toward the pink-and-white circular nebula at the center of the viewer.

"I always thought that nebula was so romantic, Bronwen. It looks like a ring you could put right on your finger."

The navigator laughed. "You would need to have a pretty big finger. The Ring Nebula is thousands of miles across, but"—Bronwen winked at her—"I understand what you mean."

Raina studied the data on the screen. "That ship or pod or whatever is a long way from Earth—two thousand one hundred fifty light years away, to be exact!"

Bronwen fine-tuned her scanners. "Whatever it is, what we are seeing is certainly very small. The scanners can barely detect it."

Raina's eyes strained to find the blip on the screen. "You must have better eyes than I have. Now I can't see it at all."

Bronwen pointed to a minuscule flicker of light. "It's right there, drifting just east of the star Sheliak."

Raina studied Sheliak on the viewer. "Sheliak is a double star—I know that much. And each star is hundreds of times larger than Earth's sun."

"You're right. And those two giant stars revolve around each other every twelve days, making the approach of any spacecraft very perilous," Bronwen stated matter-of-factly.

"And if this is an escape pod, whatever do you suppose a ship was doing out there in the middle of nowhere?" Raina asked curiously.

Bronwen ran her hand through her hair as she pondered the Ranger's question. "I'd better contact Captain Edge," she said and reached for the communications switch. "The *Daystar* may need to go on a rescue mission."

Jerusha Ericson was in uniform, but before reporting for duty she decided to check on Mei-Lani Lao in sick bay. She had been visiting her daily since Mei-Lani came down with her strange illness.

Jerusha could get into sick bay but not into the quarantine area, which was secured by an invisible force field. She came as close as the force field permitted and looked in at her friend.

Mei-Lani Lao was a very pretty and petite Asian with long black hair and brown eyes. Although she was the youngest Space Ranger, her mastery of history and languages was exceptional. Time after time, ancient languages that had defied translation by the best linguist in the galaxy just opened up to her.

Looking in at her, Jerusha thought, *Poor Mei-Lani! What could have possibly caused this sickness? And what is it?*

Dr. Temple Cole, the ship's surgeon, was still running tests but had had no luck with a diagnosis yet. And Jerusha didn't like mysteries—especially ones like this, where the health of a close friend was involved. An engineering genius, she had scanned the ship for any type of virus or bacteria, and every scan had turned up negative.

"Don't come in," Mei-Lani warned. "I don't want you . . . to catch this." She turned her head to cough.

"Mei-Lani, please don't be offended, but you look just awful." Jerusha wanted to touch Mei-Lani's forehead. Her dark hair was drenched with perspiration, and her eyes were half closed. Even her skin was an unhealthy looking color.

"Don't even *think* about . . . turning off the force field . . . and coming in!" Mei-Lani wheezed on almost every other syllable. "Please, Jerusha. As bad as I feel . . . I would feel worse if I gave this to you." Her eyes were pleading.

"I know. I'm not allowed in." Jerusha felt as if she should even back away from the protective force field. "How in the world did you get whatever this is?"

"I have no idea," Mei-Lani said. "All I know is that . . . I was in the library studying ancient history . . . about the Masai culture. You know. Tara Jaleel's people. Then, I went to the training room . . . to ask her a couple of questions. I don't know if there's any connection, but . . . I'd just gotten to the door when this big cloud of gray dust . . . almost knocked me over. And then . . . that afternoon this sickness hit me like a ton of bricks."

"What's a ton of bricks? What are bricks?"

"It's an old Earth saying I read somewhere . . . I have no idea what it means, but somehow it sounds . . .

appropriate to me now." Mei-Lani coughed again. This time, deeply in her chest.

The medical officer walked into sick bay at that moment. Dr. Cole was a highly competent doctor, but up to now she didn't know the cure for Mei-Lani's sickness. She said she didn't even know what it was.

"I'm still running several tests," she said now. "Hopefully, we'll know something shortly."

"Is there anything I can do to help you, Dr. Cole?" Jerusha asked.

"Whatever this disease is, it's very smart, Jerusha. Just about the time I localize it, it changes its biochemical makeup. I believe your prayers would be the most helpful thing right now." The doctor looked at Mei-Lani, who seemed to have fallen into a restless sleep. "I'm afraid her condition is getting worse," she murmured.

"I'll spread the word, Dr. Cole. We'll all pray for her." Then Jerusha looked long and seriously at the ship's surgeon.

"What is it, Jerusha?"

"Be careful, Doctor. I can't explain it, but I'm sensing that something is very wrong here. This may be more than just a physical illness."

"What, then? I've come to respect these special feelings that you have."

"I need to talk with Bronwen first. Just please be careful!" Jerusha hurried out of sick bay and headed toward the bridge.

3

The Escape Pod

As soon as Captain Edge listened to Bronwen Llewellen's communication, he sprang into action. "I want all of the information I can get about that small craft, Bronwen," he said. "Why it is out here in the middle of nowhere and anything else you can learn."

"Yes sir. I've already been studying it carefully." Her voice was crisp and clear over the speaker. "It's definitely the shape and size of an escape pod. And that doesn't sound good, of course."

"What can you make of the pod?"

"Only that it's an ancient style."

"How ancient?"

"I would say, Captain, that this particular craft hasn't been produced for more than five thousand years."

Standing beside Captain Edge, Zeno Thrax leaned toward the screen and studied the data from the long-range scanners. "Captain, I just can't believe what I'm seeing here," he said.

"What is it, Zeno?"

"Bronwen is right. This escape pod came from a very rare ship indeed." He pulled up a schematic from the history data banks.

"Put it on the forward screen," Edge told him, heading for the front of the bridge.

Zeno did so, then joined him and pointed to the image on the larger screen. "My guess, Captain, is that it is from one of the ancient Explorer class ships."

"Zeno, you'll have to refresh my memory on that."

"These ships were designed during a period of Earth's history when humans wanted to travel to the stars but were unable—for financial reasons—to build starships such as we have today."

Thrax went up to the screen. "A long time—years even—before an Explorer was launched from Earth's moon, a cargo ship would be sent ahead to the Explorer's destination point." He pointed to the solar system of the star Sulaphat. Then he rubbed his chin thoughtfully and continued. "My best guess, Mark, is that perhaps this pod came from a disabled cargo ship—a ship that is somewhere in the vicinity of the fourth planet orbiting Sulaphat. It appears to be the only one that can sustain life."

Bronwen Llewellen came onto the bridge at that point with further information. "Galactic Command's survey ships have determined that establishing colonies anywhere in the vicinity of the Ring Nebula could be disastrous."

"Why is that?" Edge asked.

"Captain, if you will examine the two stars located to the west of the Ring Nebula . . ."

Edge looked at the spot on the screen that Zeno Thrax was indicating. "Sheliak," he said, leaning forward in his command chair.

"The Sheliak area has always been a very dangerous place to live," Bronwen continued. "Sheliak is not one star but two. Each star is several times the diameter of Earth's sun. And the magnetic attraction of these two stars for each other throws off huge streams of hot gases. Every few years, these gases build up incredible amounts of energy and then flare up in a huge burst of radiation. Much of this radiation is drawn into the Ring Nebula."

"So any explosion of radiation from Sheliak would affect life on any planets of the neighboring star Sulaphat," Edge surmised.

"Perhaps. It would depend on the direction of the energy burst. One burst several thousand years ago headed straight for Earth."

Edge squinted toward the screen. "I can't remember the history of that."

"In the late twentieth century, a burst from Sheliak smashed into Earth's upper atmosphere. Scientists estimated that the burst had enough energy to power a civilization for a billion billion years. Several satellites were forced to shut down just to protect their electronics. If it hadn't been for Earth's atmosphere, most of life on Earth would have been destroyed."

Edge was still trying to figure out the logic, therefore, of sending any kind of ship into Sheliak territory. An old spaceship's electronics would only wind up being destroyed along with any life aboard.

The navigator appeared to sense his dilemma. "I don't know why an escape pod would be in that sector, Captain. The shields on *Daystar* would protect us today, but ships five thousand years ago didn't have our shielding technology."

Zeno Thrax was busy studying the Explorer class ships on the data banks. "Captain, the Explorer escape pods were only eight feet long and twenty-four inches across." He pulled up a picture of an escape pod.

"Looks rather like a coffin," Edge said wryly.

"The thing was piloted by a tiny robot with artificial intelligence. The living occupant was placed in sort of rudimentary cryogenic sleep." Thrax adjusted a few controls. "Most of the ships themselves were reported lost, and the project was abandoned."

As the *Daystar* rocketed on, Edge suspected that many of his crew soon would be turning their attention to the phenomenon of the ancient escape pod.

Then Raina St. Clair's voice came over the intercom. "Captain, I've tried to establish communications with the pod."

"What's the result, St. Clair?"

"No answer." She hesitated, then said, "I believe that its communication links have failed."

"Can you determine why?"

"It may well be because of the age of the ship. If it's as old as the reports read, they may have malfunctioned centuries ago."

"Captain," Thrax interrupted, "the scanners indicate that power usage is minimal."

"But some power is still there?"

"Yes sir. And the person in the pod is definitely alive—frozen stiff, but alive."

"Amazing. How can that be when there is minimal energy source?" Edge asked.

"Once in the depths of interstellar space, the capsule would need little energy to maintain the extreme cold, of course. Deep space is very cold."

"Anything else, First?"

"Well, the pod's instruments indicate that it has been adrift in space for an indeterminate period."

The captain paced the bridge impatiently for some time. Paced and watched the forward screen.

As *Daystar* drew nearer the escape pod, the vessel's registration numbers became visible. Shortly after that, Zeno Thrax said, "We've finally identified the ship, sir."

"Good. Read the report."

"It wasn't a cargo ship. It was a spacecraft registered to a Galan Knowles. Knowles and his ship disappeared on a trip to the Lyra Sector."

"The Lyra Sector!"

"Yes sir. Lyra was mostly unexplored five thousand years ago. We know little enough about it even now."

Bronwen Llewellen was sitting before her screen. When the captain turned to ask her a question, he was startled to see that her face was pale. "What is it, Bronwen? Are you ill?"

But the navigator's thoughts seemed to be somewhere other than on the *Daystar*'s bridge. *She may be developing the same sickness that's got Mei-Lani down*, Edge thought. He determined to keep an eye on her. Turning his attention back to the problem at hand, he said, "First, I want to maneuver very carefully. We don't want to damage that pod."

The escape pod was smaller than *Daystar*'s escape pod. As Thrax trained the ship's spotlights on it, the captain could see that it was covered with space dust.

"Ice is covering the inside of its window," Bronwen said. Edge's navigator seemed to have recovered somewhat. She was busying herself making minute navigational adjustments.

"What are you thinking about, Bronwen?" Raina asked her, frowning a little. "Something's troubling you."

"Time often has a strange way of bringing things around."

"What do you mean?"

"Maybe I should have said that *God* often has a strange way of bringing things around. All in His good time."

"I don't understand you."

"That spacecraft is registered to a Galan Knowles."

"Yes. That's what Zeno said."

Now Captain Edge was paying close attention.

"I heard stories about Galan Knowles when I was a girl," Bronwen said. "I haven't heard his name since."

"But who is he? Mei-Lani would like to be here right now. Here comes some history, and she's in sick bay."

"Galan Knowles is said to have had a remarkable mind. He was a wise man of great influence and had exceptional leadership qualities as well. He was also a believer in Jesus Christ."

Bronwen gently rubbed the top of her navigations console. "It's sad that in the galaxy today men rely mostly on technology to help them with their needs. Don't misunderstand—it is a blessing to have the technology. The question is, In whom do men trust—in their technology or in the Lord? Galan Knowles was a brilliant man who trusted God."

Captain Edge sat listening. He knew his navigator's Christian convictions. He didn't accept them all, but he respected her.

Bronwen looked up at Raina then. "The Bible says that the fear of the Lord is the beginning of wisdom. People think technology is the beginning of wisdom, and they forget about God. They make up silly reasons why God doesn't even exist." She turned back to the viewer. "If that is Galan Knowles in that escape pod—actually, whoever is inside that escape pod—we must at least try to restore him."

The bridge crew stood by silently as the *Daystar* continued its maneuvering.

Then Raina broke the silence. "Can the frozen man really be resuscitated, Bronwen?"

The navigator folded her hands in her lap, and she sighed. "In spite of my hopes, I must be realistic. Zeno's sensors tell us that life is still present. But no one has ever survived the resuscitation process. No, Raina. After five thousand years, it is probable that Galan Knowles is now a frozen mummy."

Mark Edge had been forced to make many unpopular decisions in his career. Being captain of a space cruiser was not an easy job. Often—no matter what he decided—he would displease somebody. Sometimes he thought of himself as a politician who had to make choices, knowing that he would displease one group at the same time he pleased another. Since spotting the small escape pod registered to Galan Knowles, he had wrestled with his decision.

Finally he slapped his knee and said, "We've got to do something with that pod! Ivan, get Heck Jordan and the other Rangers. I want a meeting at once."

"Do we need *him*, sir? I could order the grunts out there. They're used to rescue operations."

"This is not a matter of 'need.' It's more like a matter of opportunity."

Ivan Petroski gave the captain a disbelieving look, then shrugged his narrow shoulders. "I'll get them all, sir." He scurried off.

Captain Edge continued slowly maneuvering the *Daystar* into position. Already the cruiser was within one hundred yards of the escape pod.

"Zeno," Edge said quietly, "I want the Rangers to bring the pod into the cargo bay."

"Yes sir."

"It will be a simple space walk. They'll just go over and bring it back."

Petroski returned and said glumly, "They're coming. And Jordan's got an idea, sir."

"Oh, no. What is it, Ivan?"

"He's been working on improving his antigravity

unit." Petroski's hands waved in excitement. "You know—that stupid thing he designed on our mission to Makon."

"Who'd forget that? It definitely didn't work."

"I know, but Jordan says now he's got it about perfected."

"He has?" Captain Edge took a deep breath. Then he patted Ivan on the shoulder. "All right. That settles it."

"Settles what, sir?"

"Heck will be the one to lead the Rangers in their mission to recover the escape pod."

The entire bridge crew acted as if a stiff cold wind had just blown across them—or as if they were now convinced that Captain Edge had gone space happy.

"Me, sir?" Heck said as he and the other Space Rangers walked onto the bridge. His face broke into a wide, beaming smile. "Thank you, sir. I guarantee I will do you a good job! Yes sir. You do not have to worry, sir. Never fear. Jordan is here."

Ivan scowled fiercely. "Oh, settle down, Jordan! I'm not convinced the captain's picking the right person."

Edge said, "It's all right, Ivan. I've decided, and I'll bear the responsibility. After all, the pod is several hundred degrees below zero. What could anybody do to spoil anything? All the Rangers have to do is bring the escape pod to the cargo bay. And since Heck has improved his antigravity unit—so he says—the retrieval will be even easier."

He turned back to Heck Jordan. "Heck, first I want you and the others to find out if there are any exterior computer hookups that we can connect to before we drag the pod into *Daystar*'s cargo bay."

"Why do you even want it aboard ship, sir?" Thrax interrupted.

"Zeno, you know we'll have to report finding this pod to Galactic Command. And they won't want us to just leave it here floating in space—not something five thousand years old."

"I only hope Jordan doesn't wind up messing the whole thing up," Ivan muttered. "He messes up everything."

Actually Captain Edge was hoping the same. He was also hoping that this assignment would get Heck Jordan more involved with the *Daystar*'s official activities. He saw potential in the boy and really wanted to see him develop into a fine star fleet officer. This experience at leadership might help. "Let's get going," he told the Rangers, as he turned to leave the bridge. "Check out your enviro- suits. Make sure they're ready to go."

Happily, Heck started to follow him.

The other Space Rangers didn't move a muscle.

Raina St. Clair cried, "Captain, this is intolerable!"

Ringo Smith added, "He'll get us all killed!"

"You guys move it, and that's an order," Edge commanded sternly.

They did, but slowly.

Quietly, Dai Bando started to whistle an old Earth song by the name of *Amazing Grace.*

Heck raced along, following the captain. Ivan trailed behind both, as fast as his short legs would go. But he kept up. They had not gotten far before Heck was breathing heavily.

"Look at him, Captain," Petroski said. "He's in such bad shape he won't even be able to make it out of the airlock."

"He'll make it all right," Edge said grimly. He glowered at Heck. "Check out that enviro-suit, and then I'll give you your specific orders."

"Yes sir! You won't be sorry, sir. I'll bring back a report that you'll never forget, sir."

Scowling, Ivan Petroski watched Heck check over his enviro-suit. "Heck, that suit fitted you before we left Earth," he chided. "Now look at you. One of these days we're going to have to sew two suits together just to make one big enough for you."

"Don't worry, Chief." Heck began examining the fittings on the suit. "No problem at all."

The boy was probably very excited, Petroski thought. He rarely got to participate in a space walk.

Then Ivan looked about the small cubicle that was the prep room. Each locker had a crewman's name above it and his enviro-suit hanging inside it. Some of the Space Ranger suits looked very small.

The other Rangers began arriving then to check over their gear.

"This ship is nothing but a nursery," Petroski grumbled. "Nothing but a nursery."

While Heck Jordan and the other *Daystar* Space Rangers made preparation for their space walk, Capt. Mark Edge was worrying. *Maybe I'm doing the wrong thing. He always messes everything up. Always. But he's got to start somewhere if he's ever going to grow up to be a man. Doesn't he?*

4

Anyone but Heck

Raina St. Clair sat in the chow hall, waiting. Soon the Rangers would be suiting up for their space walk.

She looked around, thinking that in some respects this was the most pleasant place on the *Daystar.* The tables were placed so that each one provided a good view of space. The chairs were made of soft Dernof leather. Mei-Lani had decorated the walls with Asian watercolors of lakes, mountains, and streams. Jerusha had gathered beautiful plants from every planet they had landed on, and she had placed each one in the chow hall to complement Mei-Lani's murals. The hall was just comfortable to the senses, Raina thought. It had a homelike quality.

She was sitting down to a plate of her favorite snack—melon nectar and preserves, which had been prepared especially for her by the ship's cook. The chef was named Manta. His defining characteristic was being irritable all of the time, but the crew had grown to like him anyway. And he was a fine cook.

Raina had just begun to eat when out of the corner of her eye she caught a glimpse of Ringo Smith. She watched as he came in, put some food on a tray, then began wandering from one table to the next.

Raina was certain that he was watching her out of the corner of *his* eye, without appearing to.

He's just waiting for me to say something to him, I suppose. She waved. "Ringo, come over and join me."

His face brightened instantly. He threaded his way among the tables to sit with her. "Thanks, Raina. I hate to eat alone."

"So do I. What's that you've got for lunch?"

"Oh, it's just some orange berries. I don't feel like eating anything heavy right now. Anyway, we're not supposed to eat much."

Raina looked at his plate. Orange berries looked like peeled oranges but were as small as grapes. "Can I have a sample?" she asked sweetly.

At once Ringo placed the plate of orange berries near her.

She'd known he would. He never refused her anything when she asked like that. She scooped up a handful and sprinkled them on her melon preserves. "Thank you," she said, and she spooned some of them to her mouth.

Raina also knew that Ringo admired her. He even claimed to like the hated dimple in her chin. He was definitely smitten with her, she thought. But unfortunately for Ringo Smith, his feeling was not returned.

She decided to channel the conversation in a safe direction. "What do you think about that escape pod we are tracking, Ringo?"

"Jerusha told me a little, but I don't know much about it. What do you think?"

"I was on the bridge when Bronwen told us about it."

"How come I'm never on the bridge when things like this happen?" he asked indignantly.

Raina frowned at him. "Nobody is conspiring against you, Ringo. Stop taking things so personal."

"Oh, I suppose not." He took another bite of orange berries. "Wouldn't it be something if the frozen pilot is still alive?"

"Zeno says he is. Bronwen says probably he couldn't be. That the cryogenic process has never worked."

"It's been pretty much of a failure according to all I hear about it. They're getting better with it, but back in those days it must have been very primitive."

"That's exactly what she said." Then Raina leaned forward, and her eyes grew dreamy. "But just think about that ship. Why, it could have been drifting anywhere in the galaxy during all those thousands of years. Maybe even to another galaxy."

"That's something to think about," he agreed.

"But, Ringo—" now she sat up straight "—I'll tell you something that really bothers me, and that's the fact that Heck is getting ready to boss us around on a space walk."

"I don't think it's fair, either."

All of the Space Rangers wanted to do a space walk, but the opportunity for one came very rarely. When it did come, the grunts were usually chosen.

"Did you ever hear of Murphy's Law?" Raina asked.

"No. What is it?"

"It's an old saying: 'If anything can go wrong, it probably will go wrong'—something like that."

"Well, everything that Heck gets his hands on usually goes wrong. I probably know that better than anyone else. But he *was* the captain's choice."

"He's just the wrong one to lead!" Raina said emphatically.

Suddenly Ringo smiled. "I'll bet you'd like to lead the pod rescue yourself, wouldn't you, Raina?"

"Yes. Wouldn't you?"

"Why, sure I would, and so would every one of the Space Rangers. That would be some experience—to lead a team and float free in space like that."

"Well, *I* think the captain's wrong to appoint Heck. He's just not dependable."

Ringo may have had the same thoughts, but he said, "Heck's really all right. He just needs a little guidance."

"You're his friend, so you say that. But who's going to guide him when he's out there in space? He won't listen to anybody. There's no telling what he'll do, Ringo!"

The two talked for some time about the captain's decision, but finally Ringo just shrugged his shoulders. "Well, that's the way it is when you're a star fleet captain. You have to make unpopular decisions sometimes." He seemed to want to say something else, but he didn't. He nervously tapped the table with his fingertips for a few moments. Then he said, "I need to tell you something, Raina."

"Why, what is it, Ringo?"

"You know that small statue of Shiva that I bought?"

"Yes, I remember it. And I never did like it."

"I know you didn't. Well, I gave it to Tara Jaleel."

"Good! It would have been even better if you had thrown it in the disposal chute, though. That Shiva is nothing but an idol with Satan's evil power behind it. If Tara could see what Shiva really is, she would never worship her!"

Raina St. Clair, like many girls, was highly discerning. She studied Ringo's face and then said, "No, you shouldn't have given that statue to Tara. You should have thrown the foul thing right out into space."

Ringo flushed. "You're right," he said. "But that was just like me, wasn't it? I'm always doing the wrong thing."

Raina put her hand over his. "Don't be offended, Ringo. I didn't mean to offend. We both need to live our lives for the Lord—not for ourselves or for anybody else. And I'm preaching to myself as much as I am to you right now." She stood up. Then she came around to Ringo's chair and gave him a sisterly hug.

Just then Contessa, Jerusha's supersmart German shepherd, padded into the chow hall and over to Ringo and Raina's table. Her ears were standing straight up. She must have heard their voices.

"Hi, Contessa," Raina said with a voice that was as warm as a summer breeze.

Ringo reached over and patted the dog on her shoulder.

"Ringo, I've got to check on a couple of things, and I'll meet you later during suit-up time."

After Raina left the chow hall, Ringo sat dreamily petting Jerusha's dog and feeling as if someone had given him a diamond as big as his head. He had actually been hugged by Raina St. Clair.

While the bridge crew was preparing for the Rangers' space walk, Contessa prowled around the decks.

She walked into the training room and saw Tara Jaleel performing strange motions that were hard for her to follow. Usually Jaleel would chase her out of the practice area. Today the woman hardly seemed to notice the dog's presence. One thing Contessa did sense, though—Jaleel's anger level was at an all-time high. As she watched, the weapons officer began making even quicker movements than before.

The German shepherd left the training room and trotted down the corridor to sick bay.

"Why, hello, Contessa." Dr. Cole reached down and gave her a hug around the neck.

Contessa whined and peered into the quarantine area.

"Mei-Lani's very sick," Dr. Cole explained, as if the dog could understand every word. "And I hope we find out how to help her soon. I'm afraid she's getting weaker and weaker."

Barking softly at Mei-Lani, Contessa backed away from the protective force field. Then she padded out of sick bay.

"Come back anytime," the doctor called after her.

Her next stop was the bridge, where Captain Edge was busy giving orders. Contessa loved to hear his voice. Next to her mistress, Jerusha, he was her favorite human.

The captain looked down at her. "Be a good dog, Contessa. No jumping up today—especially on me," he pleaded.

Contessa wagged her tail happily and leaned lightly against his leg.

The captain reached down and absently scratched between her ears. Then he straightened up. "What's taking them so long to get suited up?" he growled irritably. "I've had enough of all this waiting around. Let's get this space walk under way."

Smiling, Bronwen Llewellen called, "Come on over here, Contessa. No need for you to hang around that grumpy old man." There was chuckling from the other crew members on the bridge.

The German shepherd leaped over to Bronwen and contentedly lay down at her feet.

Captain Edge was still examining his decision to let Heck Jordan even go on this retrieval mission, much less lead it. In fact, a part of him was suggesting that he had made the biggest blunder of all time. But after agonizing over it, he'd finally come up with what he felt would be a good backup plan. He left the bridge and strode briskly down the corridor to the cargo bay area.

The cargo bay was meticulously laid out. Space was limited, and Ivan Petroski and Studs Cagney had developed a method for storage that utilized every square inch. The cargo containers were color coded and numbered, making it very simple to locate supplies when they were needed.

Dai Bando obviously loved working—and singing—in the cargo bay. As Edge came in, he could hear the Ranger singing even now, while he shifted some heavy equipment with great ease.

Captain Edge waited while Dai finished what he was doing.

He admired the boy. Dai had hair as black as night, eyes so black that one could hardly see the pupils, and two prominent dimples that appeared when he smiled. And at five eleven and one hundred seventy-five pounds, he was the strongest man onboard—as well as the quickest. True enough, Dai Bando might not have the exceptional intelligence and skills of the other Rangers, but he possessed outstanding physical abilities. He was also gentle and kind. He seemed never to lose his temper.

"Dai, I've got a job for you," Edge said.

"Yes, Captain. What is it?" The boy drew himself up in front of Captain Edge. He listened closely while Edge further described the mission that Heck would lead.

"Captain, I would never question your decision, but—truly—Heck's in very poor physical shape to do something like this."

"I know that, Dai. That's one reason I'm looking for a way to get him some help."

"Yes sir. I wish you could help Heck. He's very smart, but no one takes him seriously. He pretends to be important, but I think he needs to *feel* more important."

"You've hit the nail on the head, Dai. And as I've told some others—and I'll tell you in confidence—I think that in a way Heck is a genius. But geniuses can go wrong. I have one of the officers keeping an eye on him, and I want you to help him on this mission."

Dai smiled and said, "I'd be glad to do anything I can, Captain. Just tell me what you want."

His simple answer and his bright smile somehow disturbed Edge. *I don't see how he manages to be so blasted happy all the time. It looks like he'd get down once in a while—like the rest of us do.*

"I'm truly glad you asked me to do this, Captain."

"How can you always be so happy about everything? It irritates me, Dai. All the rest of us have our moody periods, but you never do."

"If that's so, Captain, then it's because of my relationship with Jesus Christ. The Bible says, 'Rejoice in the Lord always; again I will say, rejoice!' I try to do that."

Capt. Mark Edge just looked at him. He knew Dai had a religious bent, but he certainly didn't know what he was talking about.

The boy seemed to pick up on his thought. "Captain, it's something we just can't do on our own. But I've found that God really can give strength to 'rejoice' even when things are not going right."

"All right, I'll have to agree that God does seem to have done some things around here." He thought of the amazing recovery of the *Wellington* captain. "He must have helped Captain Murphy. Only God could have made such a change in a man. And I won't argue the fact that Dr. Cole's been a different person herself ever since that experience."

"Yes sir."

"Well . . ." Edge said rather nervously, for he felt

that Dai was penetrating a part of his life that he had kept very well hidden. "Anyway, I want you to stay close to Heck on this retrieval mission."

"Yes sir. I can do that."

"If he gets into trouble, you'll be there to help him."

"Yes sir. It will be a pleasure, Captain. I'll be glad to do it."

The captain looked at his chronometer. "You've got to hurry. They're already suiting up. Everybody's scheduled to debark by the midship airlock at fourteen hundred hours."

"Aye, sir." Dai Bando rushed out of the cargo bay area. He moved so fast that he was almost a blur.

I don't see how he moves like that. His speed is inhuman, Captain Edge thought. *Well, I must say I do admire the kid—even if I don't understand all this Jesus stuff yet.*

5

No Monkey Business!

Captain Edge fidgeted nervously and shot a glance at Zeno Thrax. The Rangers' positioning of the escape pod next to *Daystar* would be a delicate matter and required extreme caution.

Thrax looked up and saw the expression on his captain's face. "Don't worry, sir. I've been monitoring their progress, and everything is fine."

"So far," the captain said sardonically.

"I don't think we have anything to worry about. Heck seems to be handling it very well."

Edge fidgeted for a few more minutes. Then he called Heck on the com link. "Jordan, what's happening out there?"

"I'm—doing all right—Captain." But Heck sounded out of breath and hardly able to speak.

Zeno Thrax peered at the monitor. "What's in that *bag* you've got hanging from your waist, Jordan?"

There was no answer.

Captain Edge exchanged a worried glance with Zeno. He spoke into the com link. "Heck, this is the captain. And I want to know what's in that bag around your waist."

"Why, it's—nothing, Captain."

"You don't have a bag full of nothing! There's no such thing as nothing. *Something's* in it! I'm ordering you to tell me what it is!"

"It's just a—a few extra chips, sir. And some tools. And the antigrav unit. You knew about that, sir."

But something about Heck's tone troubled Captain Edge. "I'm giving you an order, Jordan, and the first officer is monitoring it. You do understand your orders?"

"Oh, yes sir!"

"I'll repeat them. You will not do anything—I repeat *anything*— except retrieve that pod! I want no monkey business! Do you understand that order?"

"Yes sir! I understand, sir."

"Heck, this mission has the potential to be very dangerous. I've given you a chance. See that you don't blow it." He broke the communication and gloomily looked over toward Zeno Thrax. "I may have made a wrong decision, Zeno."

This time Thrax didn't answer. He was glued to the instruments in front of him. Then, "Captain," he said, "the Space Rangers are now approaching the pod."

"If I'd sent the grunts, they'd already be back on board with the thing." Edge's tolerance for delay was almost nonexistent. "These kids are taking forever."

Thrax smiled. "It's just that the grunts have been shoving things around in space for a long time," he said. "This is the first real space-walk assignment for our young Rangers." He readjusted *Daystar*'s starboard alignment. "Mark, remember your own first time out?"

"No, I don't," Edge lied, as he leaned forward and anxiously studied the instruments. The Space Rangers were closing in on the escape pod. "It's about time they got there!"

Each Ranger was attached to the *Daystar* by a long tether. The captain comforted himself that, as long as the umbilical cord was intact, the chances of a Ranger's being lost in space were minimal. He watched Heck Jordan pressing toward the escape pod. Apparently he was determined to be the first one to reach it.

"Captain," Heck reported, when he'd arrived, "I see some controls near the pod's main hatch."

Edge was horrified to see him take a brush from his bag and start to swish away the space dust particles from the controls.

"Jordan! Don't touch *anything!* Just examine it visually. Use the camera on your helmet to record what you see, but *don't touch it.*"

"Aye, aye, sir."

As Heck bent over to put the brush back into the bag, he noticed that his dusting had uncovered a green button. *What's that green button for?* His curiosity welled up.

"Captain, there's a green button here . . ." His finger moved to press it even as he spoke.

Behind him, Dai Bando cried, "Heck, do what the captain says!"

Now Edge was yelling into the com link. "Heck! Do *not*—do *not* touch anything!"

Heck heard Captain Edge's orders clearly as his finger pushed the green button.

At once the skin of the escape pod began to glow softly. A small door near its middle section slowly opened. A tiny mechanical object about the size of a mouse's head popped into view. Then the rest of the small device emerged.

"Heck, get away from that door! Get away! Get away!" Edge was shouting.

Heck knew he was in real trouble with the captain now. But he was fascinated. "Why, it's a little robot, Captain. Can you beat that? It's no bigger than a Neuromag! It's—"

"Heck, don't touch that!" With dismay, Captain

Edge watched Heck Jordan reach for the robot. He connected with Dai Bando on com link. "Edge here. Dai, proceed with extreme caution. But grab hold of Heck and pull him away from that pod!"

Then he com-linked with Jerusha Ericson. "Jerusha, close that little door! Be careful, but be quick!" He hoped the urgency in his voice was apparent. "Then—all of you—attach the cargo tethers to the pod and pull it to *Daystar*'s cargo bay."

Heck made his way back to the *Daystar* with Dai following close behind. "I suppose you're thinking, leave it to me to mess up," he mumbled into Dai's com link.

"I don't know, Heck. You just seem to have this compulsion to do things sometimes. Things you know you shouldn't do, but you go ahead and do them anyway."

Heck wanted to feel sorry for himself. He also felt like making excuses. "So I blew it," he complained. "Life is aggravating. I had this big chance to prove myself to Captain Edge and the rest of you, and I blew it. Maybe I pressed that green button just to prove to everyone that they were right about me."

But then Heck's thoughts turned back to the robot. "But what a *tiny* robot it was," he told Dai. "It is ingenious by my standards—and very functional in design."

The robot had been shaped like a box. It had tiny appendages coming out of it in many places. The head had reminded him of a little man wearing thick glasses. Although the device was covered with micro-sized colored lights, none of them had been functioning.

Heck looked at the datacorder in his hand. He knew the captain was mad at him, but already the initial fear of his mess up had subsided a bit. He was so excited over his discovery that he decided to report the robot's voltage output. "Captain, sir," he announced over the com link, "the tiny robot—it uses nano energy."

"What!" The captain started shouting again.

Heck hardly heard him. He was thinking of the robot. He had never seen a device as old as that one.

"If I could just take it apart . . ." he breathed. His pulse quickened at the thought. "I could take the little guy apart and put it back together many times until—"

"Jordan, report in! Now!"

Aye, captain! Heck thought.

The Rangers guided the escape pod to the rear of the *Daystar*. The shape of the capsule was like that of an old-style coffin with tubing, tanks, and computer controls attached to it. The capsule had a window mounted on the top.

Heck peered in at the frozen face inside. He was barely able to see through the crystal-covered glass. The eyes were closed, and the face was white except for the skin around the eyes, nose, and mouth, which was beet red. But Heck was satisfied that it was actually a human being within the escape pod. As he looked down, he saw a lone blue LED flashing slowly on the computer controls of the capsule.

"Sir, I'm looking in at the pilot," he reported. "He's definitely frozen—though he does have some color in his face." He started to rub ice crystals off the dials and meters. "There's no way to tell if he's alive, though."

"The best thing we can do now," Captain Edge said to Zeno Thrax, "is to float the pod into the cargo bay and take it back to Galactic Command for scientific study."

"I think that would be wise, sir. This is something

of tremendous historical importance!" Zeno sounded the alarm, warning the waiting grunts that the cargo bay hatch was about to open.

"I'm sure Commandant Lee will want this analyzed by Galactic Command's experts."

Edge and Thrax watched as the escape pod hung motionless in space under a million pinpoints of light. Then the grunts began pulling on the tether lines attached to the pod. Carefully, they drew the capsule into the cargo hold.

Then the captain—with a great sense of relief—watched the Space Rangers themselves enter the docking bay.

Oblivious to the escape pod recovery, Tara Jaleel was in the training room enhancing her Jai-Kando movements and sharpening her skills into flawless perfection. She felt one with Shiva today. It was a feeling she had longed for all of her life.

"Captain Edge to Jaleel!" the training room speaker announced.

"Jaleel here."

"Report to the cargo bay. We're bringing in the escape pod, and I need security in place when it arrives."

"Aye, Captain." Never stopping for a second, Jaleel did back flips around the entire perimeter of the training room. Then she barked orders into the com link, grabbed a towel, quickly wiped herself down, and left for the cargo bay.

"Bridge to Captain Edge."

"Go ahead. I'm headed to the cargo bay."

"Commandant Lee has responded to our call."

Edge stopped in his tracks and ran back the way

he had come. "Pipe the commandant's signal to my quarters. Security encrypt this communication."

"Aye, sir."

As the door iris opened to his quarters, Captain Edge could see the face of Commandant Lee already on his viewer. She was a small woman with gray hair and eyes. Edge knew her well enough to know that she was a formidable person and Galactic Command's most outstanding leader.

She smiled. "Captain Edge, you have a worried look on your face. How can I help you?"

"Have you ever heard of a man called Galan Knowles, Commandant?" he asked respectfully.

The commandant looked down at her console, adjusted some switches, and then looked back up at him. Her face was unchanged and showed no sign of emotion whatever. "What exactly do you know about him?" she replied.

What a poker face, the captain thought. *What is she thinking?* "I know very little, except that he is supposed to have lived over five thousand years ago. He's said to have had exceptional intelligence and leadership abilities. An escape pod registered to him is being brought aboard the *Daystar* even as we speak."

Commandant Lee continued to look at Edge, but now her eyes narrowed in a serious manner. "Two questions: First, is the man alive? Second, how did you obtain this information? This is classified information, Mark. It is so classified that even I would have trouble accessing his files."

"The answer to the first question is, there's some indication that Galan Knowles is still alive. But as you know, Commandant, there is no recorded survivor of cryogenic sleep. The answer to the second is . . ." Edge didn't finish. He well understood the look in Lee's eyes.

"Has anyone actually touched the escape pod?"

"Of course, Commandant. All of the Space Rangers were involved with bringing it aboard."

"Any out of the ordinary incidents happen?" Lee inquired, saying her words carefully.

"Only one. Heck Jordan disobeyed orders and depressed a button located on the exterior of the pod and . . ." His voice trailed off, and he frowned. He would deal with Heck Jordan later.

"And what else?"

"A small door on the pod opened briefly, and Heck reported that a tiny robot, no bigger than a Neuromag, appeared. Jerusha managed to push the door closed again."

"Captain Edge, you must be careful with that robot. I know it's tiny, but you must keep it confined in the escape pod."

"I can't help but be curious, Commandant. What's the danger?"

"I can't give you that information at this time." Lee turned and spoke to an officer. Then she focused her attention back on Edge as the man left the room. "Needless to say, I'm ordering the *Pegasus* to change course to rendezvous with *Daystar.*"

The *Pegasus* was a Magnum Deep Space Cruiser and the pride of the fleet. Twenty-four of the big Galaxy Class ships had been built for Galactic Command, and the *Pegasus* was Commandant Winona Lee's flagship.

The commandant's cruiser was more than twenty stories high, seven hundred meters long, and three hundred meters from port to starboard. She was divided into three sections: the bow, the fuselage, and the engine section.

A large bubble atop the bow was the bridge area.

Her forward section hung low like a giant upside-down skyscraper. It was full of sensor arrays, turbo cannon, and the primary communications array. The fuselage, connecting the bow with the stern, was only fifty meters across but was three hundred meters long. The aft engine section was designed as a cube and was half the size of the bow. This area housed the main reactor, aft sensor unit, and deflector shield generator. The ship's engines were the largest known to exist.

Commandant Winona Lee looked to be studying the star chart on her viewer. "I'll rendezvous with you twenty parsecs to the east of the galactic plane near the Ring Nebula." She tapped a stylus on the console in front of her. "I can only tell you this, until I confer with the Galactic Council: Our history data banks indicate that Galan Knowles was an exceptional man indeed. Some historical records indicate that he was active in a planet-wide cult movement on Earth. Others report that he was the outstanding spiritual leader of that age. Whether any of these reports are true or not is unknown. He did have a remarkable mind. After five thousand years, who knows what his mental powers may be."

"But his brain has been frozen."

"Of course it has. But that doesn't make any difference. You can't freeze a man's mind. His mind could possibly still be functioning even though his body is in cryogenic stasis. In any case, am I clear on this?"

"Absolutely," Captain Edge said. "We don't know what to expect—so expect the worst."

Lee ignored his comment. "Now back to question two. Who told you about Galan Knowles?"

Edge hesitated before answering. He had a feeling of loyalty toward Bronwen Llewellen, his navigator. He decided to stay quiet.

But the commandant's face became stern. "This

situation is too severe for any loyalties you may feel you have." She thought for a moment, looking at Edge's face. "Mark, I understand how you probably feel. But I want you also to consider *all* your feelings of loyalty. There's loyalty to yourself, loyalty to your family, loyalty to your friends, loyalty to Galactic Command, and finally, loyalty to God and His creation. Sometimes these loyalties get very mixed up." She straightened the sleeves on her tunic. "Believe me, if this person can find out about Galan Knowles, certain other people—ruthless people—will have found out, too."

Edge reflected on what the commandant had said. "It pains me to reveal this, but Bronwen Llewellen learned about Galan Knowles many years ago. She said he had unusual wisdom and leadership ability—was 'unusually gifted by God,' she says. All these years, she'd never given him any more thought until we discovered the escape pod registered in his name. Then she remembered."

The captain decided to become humorous. "I think there is a conspiracy movement afoot, whose only goal is to find Galan Knowles. Sunday school kids for the last half of the century have been working tirelessly to discover the location of a frozen man in an escape pod."

"I understand your skepticism, Captain, but you'll change your tune when you are more fully informed." The commandant was about to sign off when she warned, "Mark, guard the pod and its contents closely, but leave it alone. *Leave it alone!* Wait for my arrival." Lee's face faded from the viewer.

Tara Jaleel was headed toward the cargo bay. On the way she met two of the cruiser's grunts, who handled most of the manual labor jobs aboard ship.

"Hi, Lieutenant," one said as she approached them. "We just secured that old escape pod in the cargo bay. That thing must be two hundred degrees below zero."

Jaleel asked curtly, "Who's guarding the pod temporarily?"

"No one from security was there when we left."

Tara felt her face burn with instant rage.

"Is something wrong?" the other grunt asked.

"We must secure the escape pod immediately! Even when it is on *Daystar*. Come with me. Both of you."

Lieutenant Jaleel and two grunts had just sealed off the area surrounding the escape pod when Ivan Petroski walked in.

"Jaleel, we had to store quite a few cargo containers on the top racks over there by the door." He pointed to them. "Do you have enough open area here for security?"

The lieutenant swiftly surveyed the cargo bay and said, "No problem, Petroski. Everything looks fine to me."

"Well, those top containers are not tied down. Although I don't think they'll go anywhere. Just be careful."

The escape pod had been on board for an hour before Captain Edge could break free from responsibilities and start for the cargo bay. On his way, he met Ivan Petroski coming down the main corridor.

"You and Contessa out for a walk, Captain?"

Edge stopped and turned around. Jerusha's dog had been crawling along at his heels, close to the deck, in German shepherd style. Her black ears were pointed straight up, and her tongue was hanging out. He could tell that she was in a good mood. And that usually meant trouble for the good captain.

Edge sighed. He hadn't known that she was following him. "Contessa, find Heck," he said. "Find Heck . . . he has a candy bar for you."

Contessa didn't move a muscle. Edge rolled his eyes at Ivan and kept on going.

"Jordan, what are you doing up *there?*" Jaleel was yelling as he reached the door of the cargo bay. He stepped inside and looked to the left of the door. He saw the lieutenant, and he saw what she saw. There was Heck Jordan, balancing on top of some stacked-up cargo containers.

"I'm just looking for my toolbox," Heck called down. "The grunts buried it up here somewhere."

"Well, watch your step. You weigh so much that, if you make one false move, the whole rack will fall over. Those containers would crush you and anybody else in their way."

Then Jaleel lowered her gaze to the corridor door.

For one instant Edge's eyes met hers. He took a step or two farther into the cargo bay, then stopped and stared upward again. What sort of mischief was Heck Jordan into now?

At that moment, Heck lost his balance. He fell against the wall with enough force to shake the entire cargo rack. One precariously placed container on the top shelf began to tip.

Edge watched, frozen. In seconds that heavy container would plummet to the floor—right on top of him.

In the same instant he was aware of Tara Jaleel. Running toward him at full speed. Jumping high into the air. Intent on knocking him away from danger.

Edge hardly had enough time to realize that the weapons officer was diving toward him. He took a step backward, then another, and instinctively put up his arms to protect his head. He sensed something fly over his shoulder. And then, with a thunderous crash, the falling container struck the cargo bay floor in front of him.

When Captain Edge opened his eyes, Lieutenant Tara Jaleel and Contessa were lying on the deck. Both the weapons officer and the German shepherd appeared to be unconscious.

"Is everything all right down there?" Heck asked meekly.

The captain didn't take time to answer him. "Edge to Cagney."

"Cagney here."

"Bring a medical crew to the cargo bay at once. Tara Jaleel and Contessa are seriously injured."

"What happened?" The chief sounded as if he couldn't believe his ears.

"Just do it, Studs. As quickly as you can."

"Aye, sir."

"Edge to Cole."

"Go ahead," the medical officer responded.

"Get down to the cargo bay immediately."

"Who's hurt?"

"Jaleel and Contessa just saved my life but injured themselves in the process. They both appear to be unconscious."

Edge checked the Masai warrior first. "Tara. Tara, can you hear me?" Jaleel did not respond. "Well, you have a pulse, and you're breathing," he said to her. "Dr. Cole is on the way." He had no idea if the weapons officer could hear what he was saying.

Then he knelt by Jerusha's dog. Contessa was breathing, but she too was insensible. He lifted her left front leg a few inches, and it just fell back limply to the deck. "I'd better leave you alone, girl. Your back might be broken. Dr. Cole will be here in a minute to take care of you too." Tears stung his eyes. "I've treated you so badly, and now you just saved my life." He continued to gently rub her muzzle.

Then he reached for the com link. "Edge to Thrax."

"Thrax here. What's going on down there?"

"I'll tell you in a few minutes, although I don't exactly understand what happened myself. It's got something to do with Heck Jordan, though. Naturally. Prepare *Daystar* for immediate departure."

"But, Captain—"

"Just do it, First." Edge rubbed the moisture from his forehead.

In minutes, Temple Cole was there, kneeling beside Tara Jaleel with her medical scanner. When she finished with the lieutenant, Studs Cagney and the medical crew carefully placed Jaleel on a stretcher and carried her off. Then the doctor got busy with Contessa.

"One of the cargo boxes was falling," Edge explained while she worked. "Jaleel jumped to push me away. Contessa must have mistaken her rescue effort as an attack on me. The dog's protective instincts came alive, and she leaped at Tara. The box barely missed all of us."

"Tara apparently doesn't have any broken bones and seems to be all right except for being knocked out. I'll visit her in sick bay in a few minutes," Dr. Cole advised him.

Edge looked at his capable ship's surgeon. He'd never seen red hair and violet eyes look so good.

6
The Mystery Ship

Dai stood at the rec room port and looked out at the stars. Space walking had been a delightful experience indeed. He hadn't wanted to hurry back inside. There was something about floating in space with no pressure of gravity pulling one down that was great fun. He'd spread his arms and just floated around at times, giving himself tiny adjustments by the jets of the enviro-suit. In space all around him, millions and millions and millions of stars shone. As he floated effortlessly, he'd thought of the Scripture that said God knew the names of all the stars.

Well, if He made them all, he thought, *then it would be an easy thing for Him to know their names. Maybe someday in heaven we may learn what all these stars are called.*

On impulse, Dai turned from the port and headed for the cargo bay. He wanted to take another look at that escape pod.

But when he was almost to the cargo bay door, he stopped. An angry voice sounded from inside the storage area. It became clear to Dai that Captain Edge was having a heated discussion with somebody. He drifted closer.

The captain sounded very cross. "I don't know why I put up with you, Jordan! Do you *ever* consider the consequences to anything?"

Dai reached the doorway.

Heck wasn't smiling and was looking toward the

deck. "Sure, I do, Captain. It's just that—that sometimes things don't work out like I expect . . ."

"Young man, I'm the captain of this ship, and you *will* obey my orders. Otherwise, I'll restrict you to the nice, safe confines of a security cell until I can drop you off at a command base somewhere."

Heck Jordan was as white as a ghost. Dai was sure Captain Edge had never talked this strongly to him before. "I promise to obey your orders, sir," Heck said respectfully.

"Good. And I'll hold you to your word." Then the captain scowled up at the cargo containers stacked high on the racks. "What were you *doing* up there, anyway? Someone could have gotten killed. I nearly did!"

"I was looking for my special toolbox when I slipped."

The captain's mood seemed to lighten just a little. "Heck, I know you and your tools have saved us several times. But please, please—*be careful.* When Ringo falls, nothing happens. I don't mean to insult you, but you're a big guy, Heck. When you fall down, the whole ship shakes."

Heck reddened. He always made light of his weight, because he enjoyed eating so much. "I'll do better, sir. Dai has been trying to help me with my exercise and diet, but I sneak behind his back sometimes . . ."

Dai walked in then and put an arm across Heck's shoulders. "I'm sorry—I couldn't help hearing. Captain, I'll work harder to help him."

"Great!" Edge started to turn away. Then a danger signal must have lit up in his mind, for he turned back to Heck. "Just so there'll be no mistake, I am giving you a direct order, Mr. Jordan. Do *not* touch the escape pod. Do *not* touch the escape pod. Do you understand my order?"

"Aye, sir," Heck replied.

"Carry on." He turned his back on them and headed out into the corridor.

Heck slumped onto a nearby cargo container. "That was the worst one yet," he muttered.

Dai patted his friend's shoulder with true affection. "Don't let it get you down, Heck. It was hard, but learn from it. The captain's orders have to be obeyed. Use this dressing down he gave you as an incentive to do better."

Heck looked up. "Dai, we're just about as opposite as it gets. My problem is that I don't know how to get from being me to being like you."

Dai was embarrassed. "I'm nothing special. Believe me, if I were as smart as you are with electronics, I don't know if I could handle the brains as well as you do."

"But you're somebody special to everyone aboard this ship." Heck pushed his red hair back from his forehead. "I've never heard anyone say a negative word about you. But I hear negative words about me all the time. Every day, somebody goes out of their way to point out my faults to me. The only thing I can do is make a joke out of everything."

"Joking doesn't work." Dai replied earnestly. "If you don't take yourself seriously, then it's hard for others to."

"I don't know what to do. And if I don't change, Captain Edge will throw me off the ship. I know he will."

"Heck, I want to help you. In fact, we can all help you. But for us to help you, you have to do the 'W' word."

Heck thought for a moment. "Oh. You mean Work."

"Exactly. What you need to learn is self-discipline. That takes *work*."

"It doesn't look like it's much work for you."

"It's a lot of work for me. The talent God has given me is physical ability. I don't have brains like the rest of you, so I work as hard as I can with my body."

"You mean you work hard because you don't have brains?" Heck was looking down at his great girth.

"No . . . well, maybe at first I did, but I try to work hard for the Lord. I do the best I can to honor Him. Heck, we've all tried to talk to you about Jesus, and you still don't get it. He's real. He loves you. He died in your place. He's the one who gave you your incredible intelligence. It's His gift to you. All we've got comes from Him. Anything that we happen to accomplish in this life, we owe to Him. The Bible says that all things are from Him. All things means—all things!"

"Dai, I really do appreciate that God is important to you. But to tell you the truth, I don't see how a God who loves me could let happen some of the awful things that have happened to me—or the awful things that have happened to other people." It looked as if Heck was being as honest as he had ever been in his life. "Mei-Lani is very sick. Why did God let that happen?"

"I don't have an answer for you, except that no matter how bad it looks, God promises that all things work for the good of His children. Mei-Lani is His child, and He knows what He is doing," Dai answered.

"So I'll give you another example." Heck's mind was speeding up. "Why did God let Galan Knowles—a man Bronwen said loved Jesus—stay frozen in space for five thousand years?"

Dai shrugged his shoulders. "I don't know the answers to many of these kinds of questions. But God does what is right. Always. And you're missing the whole point, Heck."

"OK. I'll bite. What am I missing?" Heck asked with a touch of sarcasm in his voice.

"You're missing the fact that God is a God of love and mercy and justice. He wants to help people through their troubles. There's good in the world, and there's bad too, Heck. He let the world get that way for a purpose. Again, He does what's right, even though we can't understand it all."

Heck scratched his cheek. "Well, if I were God, I would only have let there be good in the world."

Dai smiled. "If you were God, and you made sure there was only good in the world, then Heck Jordan would never have had any choices."

"What are you saying?" He looked puzzled.

"In order for a person to have free choice, there have to be good things and bad things to choose from. If all there was was good things, then the only thing a person could choose would be good things! God is good, but He wants us to *choose* Him, using the gift of free choice. This is what makes our choice for Him so valuable."

Dai sat down next to his friend and contemplated how he should continue. *Lord help me say the right words*, he prayed. "Troubles happen to everybody," he began.

"That's just the problem. If God is really a good God, then why doesn't He change things? If He's God, He could make it so no one would ever have trouble. He could do something to keep us all out of trouble, and He doesn't. No, thanks. I like you a lot, Dai, but I don't need a God like that," Heck stated with much conviction. "You and Raina and the rest—look at your own lives. It looks to me like you have even more problems than people who aren't Christians."

Heck stood up. "The people who look happy to me are the rich people. They have fun and get to do what they want, when they want. They don't have to live by the same rules as the rest of us do. I admire them, and my plan is to be rich someday. Right now that's *my* free choice."

Dai understood where Heck was coming from, and he thought, *God lets us exhaust all of our possibilities so we have nowhere to go but to Him for help.* Heck Jordan's day would come.

So Dai grinned. "I think we need to get up to the chow hall. Our next order of business is to modify your diet."

Heck groaned in dismay.

"Not all at once. We'll modify it a little at a time," Dai assured him.

Heck shook his head as he went with Dai toward the chow hall. "I'm dead meat," he said.

Ringo and Raina stood just outside the sick bay, which housed Tara Jaleel, still unconscious, and Mei-Lani, still mysteriously ill.

"Raina, what do you think happened to Tara?"

"It looks like she hit her head on something very hard." Raina adjusted the collar on her tunic. Then she said, "Have you noticed that she has been acting a little strange lately?"

"No stranger than usual. Except that she ran Heck and me off the other day." Ringo poked his finger lightly against the quarantine force field. The field made a grating sound.

"Stop that! It sounds like chalk scraping against a chalkboard. You'll wake up Mei-Lani."

Ringo's face turned sheepish. "Sorry," he said and stuck both hands in his pants pockets.

Raina continued. "Everyone knows Tara Jaleel has a short fuse when it comes to you and Heck—especially Heck."

"I know, but this time was different somehow."

The entry door opened behind them, and Dr. Cole hurried in. The door iris closed, and she came directly to the protective force field and looked in at Mei-Lani.

"Hi, guys," the doctor greeted them.

Raina admired Dr. Cole and thought that she was beautiful. Temple Cole had given her life to Jesus on their mission to the Rainbow Nebula, and that made Raina feel even closer to her.

Both Space Rangers said, "Hi," back to her at the same time.

Then Raina watched Dr. Cole point her medical scanner in the direction of Tara Jaleel. "How's Tara doing?"

"I think she'll be all right. She took quite a blow from Contessa. My best guess is that they collided head to head in midair."

"But she's still unconscious after such a long time. Doesn't that mean something's wrong?"

"Sometimes, yes, but I think not in this case. Remember reading about the boxing matches they used to have back in Earth's history?"

"I read about those," Ringo said. "In fact, I've seen some of those fights recorded on data chips. If one boxer knocked out the other boxer, he won the fight. I don't know why they would call that 'boxing,' but what I saw was really interesting."

Raina laughed at his enthusiasm. "It's just like a boy to enjoy watching something like that."

Temple put her arm around Ringo's shoulders. "Don't feel bad, Ringo. A lot of people enjoyed boxing back in the olden days. Did you know that there are still planets in this galaxy that promote that sport today?"

"I've heard about that. I thought of going to a boxing match one time. But it's one thing to watch a fight on a data chip and then to watch a real one in person."

The doctor made a couple of adjustments on her scanner. "That's true with any kind of violence. Imagining it is very different from seeing the real thing." She put the scanner back in her pocket. "Anyway, when one of the boxers was knocked out, most of the time he would recover just fine. That's the case with Tara, I'm sure. It's just that, instead of being knocked out with a gloved fist, she was knocked out by Contessa's hard head. Otherwise, she is fine, and her scans are completely normal."

"Can't you do something to bring her back to consciousness?" Ringo asked Dr. Cole.

"Sure, I can, but I think she'll be coming out of it by herself shortly."

Raina looked in the direction of the force field again. "How's Mei-Lani doing?"

Dr. Cole sighed. "As near as I can tell, she contracted something—and I don't know what—when she breathed in that dust near the training room. Others breathed it, too, but apparently Mei-Lani was especially susceptible to something. I need to get information from Tara Jaleel about the Shiva statue. Fortunately, Mei-Lani's body is a fighter in its own right. I hope to have some answers today."

Raina gazed with sadness at her younger friend, who was in a deep sleep within the quarantine cubicle. *Lord, please help Mei-Lani*, she prayed silently.

On the bridge, First Officer Zeno Thrax carefully monitored operations as Captain Edge watched. The *Daystar* was powering up, and it was an anxious moment.

"Five thousand years that escape pod's been out here. How many things have happened since then?" Thrax muttered. He let his thoughts go back to the time when he himself had been just a boy in the mines of his native planet, Mentor Seven. A lot had changed since *then.*

The mines of Mentor Seven housed an albino race. These people lived deep in the bowels of the planet, heating by nuclear power. They never saw the sun. All of the inhabitants were pale, and Zeno remembered the first time he saw people not from his own planet. He had thought they looked awful with their red lips and rosy skin and different-colored hair. His lips curled up slightly as he now thought, *What must they have thought of us? We must have looked like pale worms to them.*

Suddenly something the first officer saw on the monitor interrupted his thoughts. He straightened up. "Captain!" he said urgently.

"What is it, First?"

"Look!" Zeno pointed toward the monitor. "That isn't a Magnum Deep Space Cruiser, but it's something almost as big."

"Where?"

"That's funny. It was there a moment ago." Zeno checked the scanners. "It must have disappeared inside the Ring Nebula. Maybe it's a science ship. They come through here once in a while."

"Keep an eye out for it," Edge said, and he started to rub his left hand. "When my hand starts itching, it means trouble."

Captain Edge and Bronwen Llewellen were looking over Zeno's shoulder at the monitor when Edge felt something push against the back of his leg. He spun around. "Contessa." His facial expression was one of great appreciation. "Are you all right, girl?"

"Her ribs are badly bruised, but she'll be fine. I couldn't keep her in sick bay." The ship's surgeon had a big smile on her face.

Edge, Bronwen, and Thrax turned immediately back to the monitor.

Their concern wasn't lost on Temple Cole. "What's up?"

Thrax said, "We have an unknown ship in the nebula." He pointed at the viewer. "I think it's a science vessel, but I don't know for sure. I can't think of any other ship that would deliberately fly into the Ring Nebula. It's a pretty hostile environment for star cruisers."

Edge, who was examining the sensor database also, asked the doctor, "How are our two crew persons in sick bay?"

"Tara's awake now and eager to get back to the cargo bay. I still want to observe her for a couple hours, though—so she's a delight to be with."

Her try at humor did not go unnoticed. Everyone on the bridge chuckled knowingly. Everybody knew how difficult the weapons officer could be.

"Better you than me," Edge said. "I just know she saved my life."

Contessa barked at him. "I stand corrected. Jaleel and Contessa saved my life. In spite of that, I just don't feel like a lecture on the virtues of Jai-Kando right now."

Contessa barked in agreement. Edge bent down to pat her.

"Mei-Lani is another matter. She is stable, but her body is still fighting off something. The medical computer is working on it right now."

"Keep after it—as I know you will. The answer is somewhere."

"Well, I've got to get back to sick bay," Dr. Cole said.

Captain Edge looked around at her. His face had a grin on it as wide as the Cheshire cat's. "Have fun with Tara."

7

Message from the Commandant

"Course plotted and laid in, Captain." Bronwen Llewellen swiveled her console chair in Edge's direction.

The captain acknowledged her and then turned to Zeno Thrax. "First, engage Star Drive engines."

"Shouldn't we engage them gradually?" the first officer suggested.

"No, First. I'm nervous about this mystery ship. I don't know who's in the nebula, and I don't want to wait to find out. We're out of here."

Warning signals like a multitude of bells and whistles echoed out of the klaxons. Captain Edge had ordered immediate Star Drive. But it would take several moments for the inertia control computers to compensate for the quick jump the engines would make into star speed. Until the inertia was stabilized, the crew would undergo debilitating G forces, so they all needed to be strapped into their assigned seats. Each department would report to Zeno Thrax when its crewmen were ready for the jump.

Outside the ship, the powerful Mark V Star Drive engines lit up the space around the cruiser. The vibrations produced by those engines caused the whole ship to shudder and shake. Power was building to full strength, while Zeno kept velocity at a standstill.

And then the last department reported in.

"All set, First," the grunt Myron reported from the security section.

"Ivan, how are the lights?" Zeno Thrax wanted word from Petroski as to how the light indicators looked on the engineering computer.

"We're in the green." Ivan's voice sounded scratchy.

Thrax turned to Edge, who nodded his head forward. Thrax pressed the velocity switch onto full power. *Daystar* blasted forward, throwing the entire crew back in their seats.

In a few moments, though, the inertia computers compensated for the increase in the cruiser's speed, and normal gravity returned to the ship.

"Am I glad that's over," Bronwen announced to all. "I'm getting too old for this stuff."

Zeno Thrax got up from his seat and turned around. His transparent lips were still flattened out from the G force.

Edge laughed. "First, if you ever decide to change professions, you could become a leading actor in horror movies."

Several of the bridge crew laughed, too. Their own faces had turned back to normal very quickly.

"Very funny, sir." Zeno sounded like a hissing snake.

"I'm sorry, Zeno. You're scary to look at even without the G force look."

Thrax bowed. "Thank you, thank you all very much!" he hissed at the crew.

Then Captain Edge turned all business again. "Departments report in to Mr. Thrax. Bronwen, let's recalibrate our course and heading."

Dai Bando had suffered the least of the Space Rangers when the ship exploded forward. With his tremendous short reaction time he had caught himself, but the others had been slammed back against their seats by the rear bulkhead when the ship's engines propelled them into Star Drive. All except Heck Jordan.

When the G force subsided, Heck was crawling around on the floor, complaining and blaming everyone except himself.

Raina said, "Will you hush, Heck! More than once, you've been told to strap yourself in your seat before takeoff."

Heck grumbled, "You think you know everything, Raina. I had no control over what I was doing. My body became a flying projectile."

Ringo muttered, "A flying elephant is more like it."

Dai interrupted their quarrel. "Is everyone all right?" he asked.

"Everyone looks OK," Raina said as the others got out of their seats. She helped Ringo to stand steady.

"Anyone hurt?" Dai asked again, helping Heck off the floor.

Heck complained loudly. "Whoever designed this ship needs to be hung up by the thumbs. I almost got killed."

Raina was short-tempered. "You had as much to do with *Daystar*'s refit as anyone here. If anyone's going to be hung up by the thumbs, it's you!"

Heck's voice was barely audible. "Ringo, you can have Raina back. I don't want her anymore. She's yours, buddy."

Raina was fingering a bump on the back of her head where she had slammed into something. Ignoring what she just heard, she glared at Heck and said, "If you had studied anything at the Academy about ship construction and space history, you would know what happened."

"Well, I didn't study all that stuff. I was too busy learning about circuit boards."

Jerusha watched Captain Edge, Zeno Thrax, and Bronwen Llewellen hurry to replot the course of *Daystar*. Bronwen's forehead was creased in a frown.

"What's wrong, Bronwen?" Edge asked.

"Nothing, sir."

"I can tell that there is," he said sternly. "Tell me what's going on."

"Well, the truth is, Captain, that we are very near the Ring Nebula. That worries me a little."

Jerusha remembered that the Ring Nebula was positioned between Sulaphat to its left and Sheliak to its right in the Lyra Sector. "The names of these two stars—Sulaphat and Sheliak—they're so unusual," she said.

"They were named early in Earth's history," Bronwen said. "In Arabic the name Sulaphat means 'Tortoise.' Sheliak means 'Harp.' The first civilizations of the Middle East and India named this constellation Lyra, which means 'The Vulture.' The Lyra constellation is unique in that it is the location of double double stars in the northwest quadrant."

"But what is it that makes the Ring Nebula so dangerous?" Captain Edge asked.

Bronwen brought the Ring Nebula up on the forward viewer. "See those two stars in the middle of the Nebula—in the background?"

"Yes," Jerusha said. "It's a very beautiful nebula."

"Those stars throw off the gas that makes up the nebula—making it look like a smoke ring from Earth's telescopes. Out here, it's easier to see that the nebula has more of a pipe shape. From Earth you just see the end of the pipe."

"It's awesome, for sure," Edge said. "Awesome—and very dangerous."

Tara Jaleel and Dr. Cole came onto the bridge then, and Contessa let out a deep growl.

"Tara is fine now," the ship's surgeon announced. "She has been given a clean bill of health."

"Captain," Tara said respectfully. "I do apologize. I meant well, but I could have killed you."

"Are you really all right?" Edge asked. He extended his hand, and Tara Jaleel shook it heartily. "Welcome back, Tara. But I must confess, I probably will have nightmares about your rescue attempt for the rest of my life. You wouldn't believe how fearsome you looked!"

Then Captain Edge turned to the navigator. "Bronwen, Zeno and I are going to do a little engineering to see if we can squeeze a bit more power from this ship. It will also give me a chance to examine the escape pod more thoroughly myself."

"I think that would be wise, sir," she replied.

Tara Jaleel said evenly, "And I'll head down to the cargo bay to make sure everything's in order." She left the bridge, not waiting for a reply.

Jerusha and Contessa returned to Engineering, where the German shepherd lay at her feet. The dog was still a little careful with her bruises and seemed glad to be next to Jerusha.

After a while, Bronwen Llewellen came along and looked over her shoulder. "How is the problem coming?"

Jerusha was the engineering expert. She could "fix anything," but she said, "We're still not getting any increased power from the ship, Bronwen—whatever the problem is."

"I suppose," Bronwen murmured, "all we can do is wait. The men are working on it."

Then Jerusha said, "Bronwen, Raina told me that you know a few things about this Galan Knowles."

"Yes," she said quietly.

"Can you tell me some of it?" Jerusha asked.

"All I know are stories I heard from one of my friends." A thoughtful look came into Bronwen's eyes. "Apparently, the man had a remarkable mind combined with the gift of leadership. He always credited God for his abilities, however. He became perhaps the greatest spiritual leader of his century."

"But he became a space explorer. Why did he leave Earth?" Jerusha asked.

"History is unclear at this point. One thing about Galan Knowles's life is for sure, though—people either loved him or hated him. Of course, that's one thing having a living relationship with the Lord can do for you. People get polarized. One minute you're a hero, and the next they want to crush you. Unfortunately, this often happens to folks who desire to do good for others. They are often ridiculed and misunderstood."

Bronwen scrolled down the database. "One who has a living relationship with Jesus is a sweet fragrance to some and the smell of death to others." She hit a switch on the navigations console. "If history is right about Galan Knowles, he had many enemies indeed."

For the next hour, Jerusha and Bronwen checked and rechecked all the inertia control circuits.

Once, while they were working, the navigator smiled faintly and asked, "Can you imagine what a grown-up Heck would be like?"

"Terrible, that's what!" Jerusha cried. "He's incorrigible!"

"Believe it or not, apparently when Galan Knowles was young, he was a lot like Heck is today. The man was a genius at microelectronics."

"I don't think just being a genius automatically classifies anyone in the same category as Heck!"

"You're right about that. But from the stories that are told, he sounds a whole lot like Heck to me." Bronwen leaned on the console. "Think about it. If Heck grew up without changing his behavior, who knows what mischief he could cause? He's dangerous enough as he is now!"

"I expect Heck's somehow at the root of all this power trouble we're having right now," Jerusha said snippily.

"Oh, I wouldn't be too quick to place *all* the blame on Heck."

"What else do you know about Galan Knowles?" Jerusha asked.

"One thing I'm afraid of is that, if he's really been drifting in space for five thousand years, he may have become incurably insane. Can you imagine not having anyone to talk to for that long—to be frozen and isolated but still able to think?" Bronwen looked through the portal at the Ring Nebula. "The report also revealed that he was a very handsome man and was physically as strong and active as Dai."

Jerusha smiled. "That would be something to see."

"And, according to history, at the beginning Galan Knowles was interested in the same things in life that interest Heck."

"You mean he wanted to get rich and have a pretty girl on each arm?"

"I do think that's how he started."

Jerusha sat talking with Bronwen and thinking and looking out at the majesty of the Ring Nebula.

The navigator said finally, "But I wonder what happened to get him stranded in space?"

"Maybe he was basically just trying to get to

another planet," Jerusha suggested, "and someone destroyed his ship on purpose. Some powerful person that he made angry." Then she changed the subject. "What is the danger of the Ring Nebula, Bronwen?"

"A rescue from there could become impossible."

"You mean we couldn't take the *Daystar* into it to help a ship in trouble?"

"If we did," Bronwen said, "we could have problems getting back out ourselves. The hypertex neutron radiation would make our scanners as blind as a bat."

"What's hypertex neutron radiation?"

"That's what makes up the gases in the nebula. This type of radiation is lethal to life forms."

At that moment Jerusha felt the increase in vibration of the *Daystar*'s engines as they boosted their output. She smiled at Bronwen, relieved.

The navigator said, "I think Captain Edge has managed to squeeze a bit more power from his ship."

"Bridge to Captain Edge!" It was Ivan Petroski.

"I'm still down below arguing with my chief engineer."

"You're going to destroy these engines!" the chief engineer himself shouted over the intercom. "You can't overload the power couplings like this." Edge was sure Ivan's face was beet red with anger. "The relays are turning color. They weren't designed for this speed."

"How long before they melt down?" he responded calmly.

"They could melt down anytime! How do you expect me to guess at something all the manuals tell you not to do?" And now he probably was pacing around in circles, throwing his hands in the air or pounding his fist into the palm of his other hand. "Blowing us apart won't accomplish anything."

Captain Edge could see that he had pushed Ivan Petroski to the limit of his tolerance. "OK, Ivan, back off the power just a little and keep a close eye on the couplings. If—and, I repeat, *if*—the couplings start fusing, back the power down more."

"Thank you, Captain. I won't let you down, but we have to obey the laws of physics."

Again the speaker in Engineering blared, "Bridge to Captain Edge."

"Go ahead, Bridge."

"Priority message from Commandant Lee coming in."

After his work with the engines, Edge needed to clean up, anyway. "Pipe Commandant Lee down to my quarters."

"Aye, sir."

Then he spoke to his first officer. "First, go to the bridge and check out our progress."

Captain Edge and Zeno Thrax got up and headed in different directions.

Up on the bridge, Ivan Petroski was reducing slightly the power and flow through the power couplings. He patted the engineering console. His engines were his best friends. "Don't you worry. I won't let anything happen to you."

The Star Drive engines sounded as if they purred in gratitude.

Edge rushed into his quarters to find that his viewer was flashing the insignia of Galactic Command.

"Edge to Bridge."

"Here, Captain," Raina responded.

"I'm in my quarters. Encrypt this message, priority code 376-xb010."

"Encrypted and funneled to your quarters. Security communication protocols enacted," said the official communications expert aboard *Daystar*.

The face of Commandant Lee appeared on his viewer. "Are we secure, Captain?"

"Fully, Commandant Lee."

"Status report," she asked very matter-of-factly.

Edge then told the Commandant everything that had happened since they last talked.

"I can give you another small piece of information, Captain. We traced the Galan Knowles's registry entry to a company owned today by Sir Richard Irons. Be careful, Mark. After your last run in with Irons, I'm positive that he will blast you to pieces if he gets the chance."

"Kind of a colorful way to say that, don't you think —being 'blasted to pieces'?" Edge said tersely.

"Mark, the metaphor isn't the problem. What's wrong out there?"

"The *Jackray* could be hiding in the nebula. If she is, she's certainly powerful enough to destroy us." Edge brushed back his hair in a nervous gesture. "Commandant, I'm not worried about me. But the thought of the Space Rangers being in harm's way gets to me. They should all be at home doing normal things." His voice sounded uncertain. "I dislike taking teenagers into action, Commandant—under *any* circumstances! And I don't see how you can expect that of me. It's bad enough when a ship loses an adult crew member, never mind losing kids. Ivan's right. They're still babies." Edge put his head down and rested his forearms on his knees.

"Mark, none of these young people ever had a normal childhood, and even if you returned them to their home planet, they still wouldn't live a normal life.

Think about it—what is normal today? The thought of losing any of the Space Rangers grieves me deeply, too. But look where you are. Your job, along with theirs, is to successfully complete dangerous missions in deep space for Galactic Command. Missions that you receive directly from me. Everyone knew this from the start. Any of you could get killed at any time. That's the sort of thing I have to live with every day. You have only your ship and crew to worry about. I have the responsibility for the whole Galactic Command."

The Commandant took a moment to compose herself. "Galactic Command needs the Space Rangers. They have no political baggage to carry around, and they have proven themselves many times over. You should be proud of them."

"I *am* proud of them," Edge pointed out. "When we went on our first mission to Makon, they were just crew members. Now they're family."

"Welcome to my world, Captain Edge. And now I have to discuss Galan Knowles."

"He's still frozen and under Jaleel's direct security watch. Not even Heck can get at him."

"Be sure you keep him frozen," Lee directed. "I want him returned to Earth so that Galactic Command scientists can try to restore him from cryogenic sleep. When and if Galan Knowles awakens, I want to be absolutely sure about what we have. There's the potential for a dangerous situation here."

"I had no idea that this situation with Knowles was so serious," Edge said slowly.

"Judging by the historical accounts, he was an unusual man before he departed from Earth. Right now, he's hindered by the cryogenic freeze. Once he returns to normal, who knows what powers he will have—or who will want access to them?"

"I wish we'd never found the man."

"Look on the bright side. Better you find him than Sir Richard Irons. Irons would use Galan Knowles's abilities for his own benefit until he ruled the whole galaxy. Then Irons would throw him away like so much garbage." Lee's eyes suddenly reflected a motherly affection toward Edge. "I care about what happens to you—all of you! You don't realize how much I trust you. Or how much I need you." She straightened. "Captain, chin up. I'll meet you at the rendezvous point shortly."

"Aye," Edge said slowly as Lee's face faded from view.

8

Toward the Ring Nebula

On the bridge of the *Daystar*, Edge was getting more and more nervous. "Look at that, First," he said. "What's wrong? We're headed straight toward the Ring Nebula."

"Yes sir, we are." Zeno Thrax was a calm individual. He was calm now. "I'm afraid that our velocity into Star Drive messed up the parameters in the navigations computer. We're compensating for that now."

Edge had never once seen Thrax rattled, and now the first officer's steadiness was surely needed. Captain Edge felt he himself was losing it.

"I should have followed your advice, Zeno!"

"You thought you were doing the right thing, sir."

"It's just that I want the escape pod off my ship ASAP. I know Heck. To have something like that pod aboard will be too much of a temptation for him. And whenever Heck touches *anything*, it either blows up or falls to pieces," the captain said with frustration.

"Or occasionally it works better than ever," Thrax reminded him.

"If that pod's here, he'll find some way to get at it."

"It won't come to that, I'm sure," Zeno said quickly.

"I appreciate your encouragement, but in a few minutes the *Daystar*'s scanners are going to be totally useless," Edge almost shouted. "The hypertex neutron radiation from that nebula will shut them down completely."

"Maybe Bronwen will be able to do something,"

Thrax said. "I understand that right now she's working with Jerusha on a systems link that will enable us to use our close-range scanners."

Bronwen gave Edge her report. "The Ring Nebula is actually millions of miles across. As you can see, there is a layer of pink gases that surround an inner white gas layer. The pink gases will disrupt our sensors, but it's the white gases that are the lethal ones. They contain the greatest amount of hypertex neutron radiation. Over time, the neutrons dissipate, turning the white gas into pink. The stars located in the center of the nebula start the whole process over again by shooting a fresh layer of white gases into the ring."

"If our sensors are down, and Irons is in there, how can we avoid him?" Edge asked. "For that matter, how can *he* see anything?"

"The *Jackray*'s engines will leave a wake through the pink gases—much like the propellers on an ocean-going vessel leave a wake on the water's surface. We should be able to see that visually."

"It would help a lot to know if that ship really is the *Jackray*," Edge muttered.

Zeno Thrax was adjusting a set of tuning controls for the front viewer. "With this—" he lifted up the device "—we should be able to see their wake easily. No matter what ship is in there."

"I hope it'll work, but we don't have much time, First," Edge said. "And if *Daystar* gets lost in this nebula, we'll be like a very tiny needle in an enormous haystack. The Commandant will never find us."

Jerusha was working feverishly on a faulty system.

"Haven't you got that fixed yet, Ericson?" he asked.

Jerusha glanced up at him. She had a rather short temper at any time, and at that particular point she totally lost it. Her face grew red, and she snapped, "What do you expect of me?"

Captain Edge also had a short temper. This did not make for a good match. "I expect you to do your job!" he said loudly.

"My job is not communications! I'm not a communications expert! Raina is the communications expert. And, unfortunately, Raina is not on the bridge!"

Captain Edge was feeling a little guilty over his own attitude or he would not have shouted back, but he was and he did. "You're supposed to get that thing fixed!"

"Heck is the electronics expert, but, unfortunately, Heck is not on the bridge, either!"

"*You* certainly aren't the expert! Well, I'm the captain, and I'm telling you to get that thing fixed!"

Jerusha shouted even louder, "And Ringo is the computer expert! Do you have any idea where Ringo might be right now? *He's* not on the bridge. This is all your fault, Captain! Whoever heard of powering up into Star Drive before the acceleration process? We're lucky we're alive."

Bronwen put a hand on Jerusha's shoulder and squeezed it tightly.

"Jerusha, that's enough," she said quietly. Probably Bronwen knew that Jerusha felt angry and that Edge was the most obvious choice for venting that anger. "You've no right to shout at the captain like that. We can't have this kind of conflict."

Tears arose in Jerusha's eyes, but she drew her lips together in a tight line. Finally, though, she seemed to get control of herself. "I'm sorry, Captain," she said. "I'm very sorry. I was totally out of line."

The presence of Bronwen Llewellen had helped Captain Edge's own nerves to become steadier. He swallowed hard, gritted his teeth, and forced himself to wait until most of his impatience drained away. "The situation is not your fault, Jerusha. And you're right. I ordered Star Drive too quickly."

The atmosphere seemed to clear at once.

"We need your skills on the bridge, Jerusha," Edge said and managed to summon up a smile. "You're the best we've got for this problem."

Jerusha flushed and smiled back. "I'll do my best."

Bronwen Llewellen said, "Captain, why don't you go have a cup of coffee and check on Ivan's progress with the Star Drive."

"That's a good idea," Captain Edge said. He knew that Bronwen simply wanted to get him out of the way, but he was ready to go. He left the bridge, saying, "Get the others up here. And let me know when the work is completed."

Jerusha turned to Bronwen and bit her lip in mortification. She said, "I just lost it, didn't I?"

"We all do that at one time or another."

"Will I never learn to keep my temper?"

"How old are you, Jerusha?"

"I'm fifteen. You know that."

"Well, I'm fifty-two, and I haven't learned it completely yet."

"You never seem to get angry."

"Yes, I do. Sometimes I get so mad inside that I want to spit. But I've learned to control my outward responses. That's what you'll learn, too, as you get older. We may never get over some of our tendencies, but we learn to control them through the Spirit of the Lord." She smiled gently and said, "The captain trusts you, Jerusha. That means something."

Jerusha Ericson took a deep breath. "Yes. That

means a lot," she said. Then she turned to the control board. "I've got to hurry with this." Turning on the intercom, Jerusha said briskly, "Raina, Ringo, and Heck report to the bridge at once."

Bronwen decided to go to her quarters. She needed a short rest. She had done so many calculations that her mind was tired.

"I will be so glad to get off the bridge and lie down for a while," she said out loud to no one in particular.

Her cabin was comfortable, almost cozy, and always had a warm peace about it. She had pictures of family and close friends displayed on the shelves and walls.

The possession that she enjoyed most—beside her Bible—was hanging on the wall next to her bed. The name of the device was "Like Being There." Bronwen thought the name was funny at first, but she'd come to appreciate its accuracy.

"Like Being There" was two feet high and three feet across and was paper thin. Using her remote, she could program a roaring fireplace fire to appear. Pressing other buttons produced a waterfall, mountain scenery, a multitude of different species of birds, a rain forest, a thunderstorm, exotic fish, or a scene that made her feel as if she were flying on top of the clouds. There was a picture for her every mood. "Like Being There" had been costly, but it had paid for itself many times over. She also appreciated the fact that whenever she was transferred to another ship, all she had to do was roll it up and stick it in her bag.

Bronwen programmed a waterfall to appear. Immediately she was viewing a slender stream of water that fell a long distance before spreading out in cloudlike fashion at the bottom. She was happily gazing at it when the door bell chimed.

"Come in," she said.

She remained lying down, expecting that her visitor would be Jerusha or Temple Cole. The person who did walk in, however, caused her to stand up immediately.

"Hello, Tara. Come in and have a seat." She motioned to a nearby chair.

Tara Jaleel sat. "I hope I'm not disturbing you," she said in a civil tone. "I won't be long. I must return to the cargo bay shortly."

Bronwen drew up another chair next to the lieutenant and sat down. "Of course you aren't disturbing me. I'm just a little surprised. I wasn't expecting a visit from you."

"Are you expecting someone else? I can come back later." Tara Jaleel started to stand.

"No, no. Sit back down. I'm not expecting anyone." Bronwen picked up the remote to discontinue the waterfall.

"Can you leave it on, please? The waterfall is soothing to me right now."

Bronwen placed the remote back on the table next to her bed. "It's soothing to me too."

Tara was fidgeting, obviously uncomfortable sitting in Bronwen's cabin. "I've been to that waterfall."

"You have?"

"The name of it is Angel Falls, and it's located in a country on Earth named Venezuela. It's Earth's tallest waterfall."

"How tall is it?" Bronwen asked.

"If I remember correctly, more than three thousand feet high. Some friends of mine hiked to it with me, and then we rock climbed to the top."

As the women watched the screen's view of the

waterfall, Bronwen commented, “That jungle looks so impenetrable.”

“It is,” Tara said crisply. “We barely made it in. The rock climb became the most dangerous part, though. One of my friends lost her life.”

“I’m very sorry.”

“She knew the risks. But the clouds at the top of the falls were very thick. She made a false move that resulted in her fall.” The lieutenant’s face displayed no emotion.

Bronwen watched the waterfall and thought, *I’ll never be able to look at this scene the same way again. I’ll always picture that poor girl falling thousands of feet to her death.*

Tara continued, “I believe that’s why I’ve come to you. The clouds in my life have become a little thick, and I don’t want to make a false move.”

“What do you mean, Tara?”

“As I’ve told you before, I’ve been a follower of Shiva all of my life. I’ve tried to make myself into one of Shiva’s most devoted servants.” She hesitated, as if not knowing exactly how to continue.

Bronwen encouraged her gently. “Just relax, Tara. Take your time.”

Tara took a deep breath, then went on. “You have no idea how hard this is for me. Just talking to you violates so many of the principles I have in my life.” Her voice sounded strained. “At the end of our last mission, something . . . happened.” Tara repositioned herself on the chair. Then she got up and began to pace back and forth in the small cabin. She reminded Bronwen of a panther pacing back and forth in its cage at a zoo.

“I was admiring my huge statue of Shiva. I had never seen one like it before, and I was proud that Shiva had allowed me to own it. Suddenly it seemed I heard the loud blast of a trumpet. I'm sure I didn't hear it with my ears but in my mind. I watched helplessly as Shiva's statue was reduced to dirt and dust right in front of my eyes. I looked about to see who was there —who could have caused this—but saw no one." Tara sat back down in the chair. "I vowed I would avenge Shiva and kill whoever had destroyed her likeness."

"That's a strong vow, Tara."

"I know, but I was furious." She cleared her throat. "It was then that I got the idea to carry out the ritual of 'Shiva's Arms.'"

"And what is that?"

"It's an ancient ritual dating thousands of years back in Masai history. Female warriors had a direct link to the spirit of Shiva. This link allowed them to move their arms so quickly that no human eye could follow."

"I see the connection." Bronwen said gently. "So you began going through the ritual . . ."

"Yes, I did. But what I didn't expect was that Shiva would speak to me. At least, at the time I *thought* it was Shiva. And not long ago, a voice spoke to me again. I thought it was Shiva. But I am no longer sure it was her voice . . ."

"Now whose voice do you think you heard?"

"This is the cloudy part for me. Part of me remains loyal to Shiva, but the other part hates lies and deception. All of my life, I've given and given of myself to my goddess. I've never received anything in return. When I finally heard her voice—or thought I did—then her statue simply . . . disintegrated."

"And so you have found that Shiva is not who she claimed to be."

"Exactly! I thought my goddess's powers would protect me. But, indeed, Shiva cannot even protect her own statue."

For the first time, Bronwen thought she saw grief in the weapons officer. "I fear that your 'goddess' has played a game with you, Tara."

"If it wasn't for Contessa, the captain would be dead right now. My well-meaning effort to save him would have killed him. I was out of control." Tears started flowing. "How could Shiva let this happen to me? Where was her protection? Her strength? Her guidance?"

Bronwen sat still in her chair. She was humbled that this Masai warrior, this expert in martial arts, would be sitting in her cabin weeping with such sorrow. After several moments, she asked, "Tara, how can I help you?"

The eyes of the weapons officer were focused on the table. Then she looked up at Bronwen. "I don't want to make a false move and come crashing to the jungle floor like my friend. Since I have been aboard *Daystar*, I have seen your God do many miracles. For example, in spite of my many years of self-discipline and rigid training, Dai Bando eludes me every time. This I attribute to the God that both of you serve." She cleared her throat. "I would like for you to pray for me. If Shiva is not the true God, but is a deceiver, I don't want to follow her anymore. Pray for me that your God will reveal Himself to me. I must know the truth."

Bronwen Llewellen took Tara's large hand in her own and clasped it firmly. Then she prayed that the Lord of the universe, Jesus Christ, would reveal Himself to Tara Jaleel as soon as possible.

9

Heck and the Green Button

Raina, Heck, and Ringo cleared with security at *Daystar*'s cargo bay door. Then they went in to have another look at the escape pod. The pod's computer console, Raina realized almost at once, was much different from the ancient one that she remembered studying in the history chips.

"Ringo," she said thoughtfully, "I have a pretty good memory, especially when it comes to communications."

He was looking over her shoulder at the pod's communications computer. "So what's up, Raina? What are you thinking?"

"That this technology here is much more advanced than the technology Earth would have had five thousand years ago. I know it is. These frequency compensators weren't even invented until much later. How could they be on this escape pod if it has been adrift five thousand years?"

"Good question," he murmured. "What's going on here?" He stepped nearer the pod for a closer look.

"Don't get too close to that green button!" Heck yelled. "Captain Edge will blame it on me if anything happens."

Raina was totally engrossed in her newest discovery. She moved over to the main viewer controls. "And look at this." She pointed to the integrated circuitry that fed into the viewer. “We had this same stuff on the first *Daystar* before it crashed. This is relatively recent technology, too.”

Just then she saw Dai Bando walk into the cargo bay. She adjusted two control switches on her scanner and called, “Dai, come look at this!”

Dai joined Raina, Heck, and Ringo beside the capsule, and all peered into the viewer.

“Does this mean what I think it does?” she asked. “This pod is warming up! These readings indicate that its internal workings have somehow powered up.”

“That’s what they indicate,” Ringo agreed.

“So what’s going to happen?” Dai asked curiously.

“It’s hard to say. Never heard of anybody ever encountering anything like this before,” Ringo said.

Heck was still busy concentrating on the circuitry. He studied the instruments with murmurs of admiration. Suddenly he announced, “Why, I’ve had most of these ideas myself. I just never had a chance to try them out!”

Ringo gave him a sour glance. “You always have ideas that you never have a chance to try out.”

Then Ringo looked back at the escape pod and scowled, and Raina could almost see the wheels going around in his head.

“It is very unusual,” Ringo said. “This is really incredible. Some of this stuff is very old, but it has been integrated into a matrix combination using technology that I’ve never seen before. Whoever put this together was a genius.”

Dai Bando seemed to be paying little attention to the conversation. He just wandered around the pod, looking at its features but touching nothing.

Raina could make no sense out of what she was seeing. But she and Heck agreed with Ringo that it was a most unusual system. And why was the pod powering up? She and Ringo stood silent, deep in thought, while Heck pushed his nose close to the control panel, still examining the circuitry.

"We really could be in danger here, you know," Ringo said abruptly. He glanced around the cargo bay. "We don't know anything about what's going on inside this pod . . ."

At that moment, Heck reached an arm across the control panel in front of them, pointing excitedly. "See that? Way over there? That's exactly what I thought—" And then he lost his balance. He fell with a thud against the console. "Oops!"

At once the pod's metal skin began to glow softly. Then a small door near the middle section of the pod slowly opened. A mechanical object about the size of a mouse's head popped into view.

"Heck! Oh, no!" Raina cried. She knew what had happened. He had bumped the green button.

There was no way to get the little door closed in time. As they watched, the miniature robot walked out and stood on the pod's exterior. The tiny robot's internal computer appeared to be running, but Raina could only guess what its multicolored light system meant. The pattern was slow and regular.

"Heck," Raina wailed. "How could you possibly have been so clumsy?"

"What do all those lights mean?" Dai asked.

She stood next to him, dismayed but fascinated. "I am just guessing, but the lights are muted, and the pattern is stable. I think the robot could be in standby mode."

Heck finally spoke. "That's as good a guess as any," he said glumly. "And I don't know *how* I happened to hit that button. I never meant to!"

"The robot doesn't appear to be hooked up to the pod's main controls," Ringo observed. "Maybe—"

Now lights suddenly started flashing in every color of the rainbow and in patterns that Raina had never seen before. The robot began to move. A multitude of sounds started emerging from the different computer systems, and air began to ventilate from the pod itself.

"What's going on?" she cried.

"It's venting gases. Use your scanner!" Ringo shouted.

She scanned the gases quickly. "It's mostly water vapor with traces of . . . antifreeze."

"Antifreeze?" the others all said.

"It's biochemical, but it's definitely some type of biologic enhancer."

Then a small scanning dish appeared on the robot's head. It was pointed in the Space Rangers' direction.

Dai swooped up Raina and ran with her around the rear of the pod. "That robot's starting to scan us," he said.

"Dai, I'm scared," Raina said.

"What of?" asked Heck, still standing beside the pod. "I can smash this thing like a fly." He raised a fist.

"Heck, stop!" Dai yelled.

As Heck's fist rose, the tiny robot projected a visible bolt of energy that threw him across the cargo bay.

"Everybody get away from the pod," Dai ordered. "We don't know what this thing can do."

Raina remembered an ancient Earth movie called *Frankenstein.* In it, a mad scientist had created a monster out of human body parts, then accidentally put in it the brain of a mad killer. She recalled how the movie had frightened her as a girl. She stared wide-eyed at the little mechanical man, wondering if any of them would live through this experience.

Captain Edge sat near the rec section of the chow hall, next to its large portals. The *Daystar* had room for only one large meeting area, and this was it. He held a half cup of cold coffee and looked down into it as he swirled it gently. Just thinking about the Ring Nebula made him depressed.

He was still sitting that way when Dr. Cole entered a few minutes later. He looked up.

The medical officer brushed back her strawberry hair with one swift movement as she put her eyes on the captain. They were beautiful eyes, large and violet with thick, long lashes. "What's the matter, Mark?" she asked quietly.

"It's just that the responsibility of this ship gets to me sometimes, Temple. Once in a while I rediscover that I'm not made out of steel. That's always discouraging."

Dr. Cole took a chair beside him. "What about this Ring Nebula? I really don't understand it."

"Well, it's certainly a strange situation. For years, scientists have tried to control the emissions from that nebula, but they've never been able to do it."

"Why? What's different about them?"

"And that nobody really knows. They don't interact with normal molecular structures. The hypertex neutron radiation would go right through our shields, then through the ship, killing every living thing."

At that moment the intercom sounded. "Bronwen Llewellen to Captain!"

"Right here, Bronwen."

"We've completed the linkup, sir. You're needed on the bridge."

A star fleet captain often does what he doesn't want to do. "I've got to go," he said.

Temple gave him a quick smile. "I'll see you later. Don't be discouraged. It's going to be all right."

But Captain Edge suspected that hidden inside the less dangerous pink cloud of the Ring Nebula was an enemy that the crew of the *Daystar* should try to avoid at all cost—the *Jackray*. He didn't mention that. He headed for the bridge.

Sir Richard Irons was the owner of the *Jackray*, a highly advanced starship. He was a brilliant engineer, his title was real, and he was immensely wealthy. What he craved was power—the power to rule the lives of the citizens of the entire galaxy. His ruthlessness knew no bounds, and he commanded a band of evil pirates who manned a fleet of fast cruisers.

Sir Richard wanted to obtain two things at this stage of his long-range plans. He wanted to know the secret location of the entire deposit of the mineral known as tridium, and he wanted the genetic brainpower of the man called Galan Knowles. He hoped to gain both very shortly.

"Sir Richard, just how far away is *Daystar?*"

"We are quite blind in here. These nebula gases are affecting our sensors, but my best guess is about two hours. I'll be glad to be out of here as soon as possible. We can't use our Stealth mode inside this cloud. When *Daystar* enters the outer boundary of the nebula, tractor Edge's ship into the cargo hold." Irons laughed. "Then we'll deal with Captain Edge. And I don't want any of Commandant Lee's deep space beacons catching us in the act."

"Yes sir."

The *Jackray* was two-thirds the size of a Magnum

Deep Space Cruiser and used the Mark IV engines. Its Interstellar Stealth technology had been outlawed by Galactic Command many years ago.

Suddenly there was a blip on the forward viewer.

"What's that, Captain?"

"I have no idea, sir. But there's its registration signal." The *Jackray*'s captain examined his sensor readings. "The ship is very large, almost twice the size of the *Jackray*. Sir Richard, it's the *Pegasus!*"

"What's her heading?"

"She's on a course to a sector twenty parsecs from here."

The plot thickens, Irons thought as he watched the ship speed closer to their position. "Captain, change of orders. Keep the *Jackray* hidden inside the nebula until we see what's going on."

"I think that's a good idea. Better safe than sorry."

"As much as I want Galan Knowles, I can't risk the *Jackray*. We can easily handle Edge and his bunch. But Lee's ship is huge, and since her armaments match her size, we'd have no chance in a battle with her."

Galactic rumor had it that Irons had installed advanced weaponry aboard his ship. But when it came to showing his moves to a Galactic Command starship, caution won out every time. If Sir Richard Irons was anything, he was a patient chess player—and a very cunning one at that.

10

The Giant Spacecraft

Captain Edge ran onto the bridge and up to Bronwen Llewellen's navigational console. "Have you had time to test the link yet?"

"Yes, Captain." Bronwen turned a control switch. "There's something else, though. And I believe you'll want to see this."

She directed him to the front viewer. The Ring Nebula became more clearly detailed than previously. Its "ring" shape was actually more like the end of a gigantic cylinder extending two million miles away from them.

"As you can see," Bronwen continued, "the device we installed is designed to reveal engine wakes in the gaseous cloud of the nebula."

Edge walked over to the viewer, looked closely at the screen, and pointed to an anomaly that appeared just inside the nebula. "This looks like a wake being generated all right. It's stationary, but it's definitely a wake from something. Are we sure that our equipment is working correctly?"

"We're sure, Captain." Jerusha spoke up. "And we both believe there is a ship parked inside the cloud. It's hanging just inside the boundary and appears to be waiting for something."

"But why would they wait? If it's us they want, then why don't they just come right out and take us?" Edge puzzled. Absently he rubbed his left hand, which was a sure indicator that the captain was nervous.

Bronwen wrinkled her forehead, then placed her right hand on her hip. "Several reasons come to mind, Captain. Perhaps it is no one looking for us. Or maybe the nebula gas emissions affect their sensors, and they don't realize how close we are to them." She tapped her finger on the navigational console. "Or they may not know who else may be in this sector, and they are therefore being cautious."

"Meaning?"

"If it is Irons, he'll want to remain hidden in the nebula, so that no one can witness our kidnapping. Irons knows that Galactic Command wouldn't stand for that."

Edge nodded his head in agreement, but his gut feeling was telling him that there was another ingredient. "Any other ideas?" he asked.

"Captain, I agree with Bronwen," Jerusha began. "I have a funny feeling that it *is* Sir Richard Irons. He probably intercepted the registration inquiry that we received earlier."

"But how could he have traveled here so fast? His headquarters are near Denebian space." Captain Edge made rapid calculations in his head. "At top speed, he would still be several sectors away."

Zeno Thrax looked as if he had been waiting his turn to speak. He said, "Unless this is all some sort of elaborate trap."

"Go ahead, First. What are you thinking?"

"I'm sure Irons wants Galan Knowles in order to further his own purposes. But I also think he wants to 'kill two birds with one stone,' to quote an ancient Earth proverb."

The captain's eyes opened wide. "The tridium!" he exclaimed. "Of course. He plans to seize the *Daystar*, kidnap Galan Knowles, and then make me tell him the secret location of Makon."

"Exactly," Zeno Thrax said.

"Exactly," Jerusha agreed.

Captain Edge studied *Daystar*'s heading toward the projected intersection point. And then he made his decision. "The *Jackray* is waiting to ambush us. I'm convinced of that. Bronwen, contact Galactic Command on an encrypted channel. Relay our current status and request the current location of the *Jackray*. Just to be safe, we need to be sure it's Irons's ship before we go in there blasting."

"Aye, sir."

Irons retired to his quarters aboard the *Jackray*. His penthouse suite was as luxurious as money could buy. No expense was spared for his creature comforts. The floor was covered wall to wall with thick golden carpet woven by the Glowsac weavers of the planet Ellak Seven.

Each wall displayed tapestries that originated in the lost kingdom of the Amesstorites. The woven pictures were the only remaining artifacts that revealed the beauty and nobility of the Amesstorite people. History gave no clue as to the catastrophe that had completely wiped out this ancient advanced civilization. Irons's pride deceived him into thinking he was their kindred spirit.

The furnishings that graced the living area were made by the most gifted craftsmen in the galaxy. Each piece told the story of the people who had crafted it.

The living room was dominated by a large sectional couch made from the white seal pups from planet Earth. These seals had been government protected for thousands of years, but that made no difference to

Sir Richard Irons. Whatever he wanted, he took. Money was no object. He firmly believed that everyone had his price.

Irons was relaxing on the couch when Francesca Del Ray, his second in command, entered the living area. Shiny blonde hair flowed down to the small of her back. There were few women in the galaxy whose beauty could compare with hers.

Irons patted the couch next to him. "Come, sit here."

He knew that his second in command was, like him, cunning and ruthless. He also knew that she especially didn't like anyone issuing commands to her.

"Is that an order, Your Majesty?" she replied in a mocking voice.

"Far be it from me to order you to do anything." Irons shifted his position on the couch. "You have the most beautiful blue eyes I have ever seen—except when you get angry. Then they turn to daggers." He patted the couch again.

Francesca Del Ray smirked. She was a vain woman. Irons knew that as well, and he had the ability to use her vanity against her.

Sitting on the couch—but not too close—she said, "You need to show me more respect."

"Why would you say that?" he asked.

"You don't listen to me."

"What do you mean? What have I *not* listened to?"

"What I have said about Galan Knowles."

"You don't understand, my dear. When I harness the power of Knowles's great mind, I'll have the power to rule Galactic Command easily. Lee and her cohorts won't be able to resist me. No one will be able to resist me."

"Galan Knowles is a legend! Nobody knows for sure what he is capable of, if anything—including you!

There's just the chance that Knowles will destroy everything that we have so long worked for."

"I've examined the records of his life. I know him better than anyone alive. I'll hire the most advanced scientific minds to properly unthaw him. And once we do that, we'll make him believe we're doing this all for him—so that he can be the wise and good ruler of the galaxy, using that remarkable brain of his."

Then Irons said, "And that's where you come in, my dear. You are my conger eel, ready to strike without warning. Then, after Knowles brings the Galactic Council to its knees, we'll rid ourselves of him."

After several moments, Francesca said, "All right. I'll play the conger eel for you, but you owe me big time, Sir Richard Irons."

"Anything, even up to half of my kingdom."

After the debilitating effects of the robot's energy beam wore off, Heck eased himself back toward the tiny robot. "Ringo," he said softly, "help me take this thing apart."

"Don't mess with it!" Raina commanded. "You know what happened before."

The robot started to move again.

Fascinated, Raina watched. "The feet are so tiny," she remarked to Dai. "It will take it all day just to get off the pod."

But then she gasped, for the unexpected happened. This robot could fly. The sight of the mechanical man rising into the air was unnerving. She and Dai, Ringo and Heck backed up as far as they possibly could. The patterns of light that shone from the robot's metallic skin were mesmerizing. Then, as they watched, the form and size of the robot changed from being a small, boxlike shape to one that resembled a full-sized human being. It stood on the deck of the cargo bay, facing them.

"Incredible!" Heck said. "What kind of metal can do that?"

"Obviously, none known to our science," Raina answered.

Ringo eyed it, full of wonder. "The robot has turned itself into a man—a silver-colored man. And"—he turned toward the others in bewilderment—"there's not a single seam anywhere on its body that I can see. How does it move around?"

For probably the first time in his life, Heck was speechless.

"Let's keep our distance," Dai warned.

The robot appeared to be looking at them. It didn't have human eyes, though. What it used for eyes seemed to be scanner lenses. Raina's datacorder could detect the robot's sensors scanning them.

Then the robot man lifted its left arm, and a panel on that arm opened.

"Look out! That's some kind of weapon!" Ringo yelled.

Indeed, what looked exactly like a weapon emerged from a slot in the robot's arm.

"There's nowhere to run," Raina whispered. "He's between us and the door. And the guards in the corridor have no idea what's going on in here."

Dai Bando crouched, prepared to fling himself against the robot. It was one of those times when his superior strength and speed and lightning reactions might get them out of trouble.

But just before Dai threw himself forward, the robot spoke. "Please stand clear of the pod." The voice was halting and contained a great deal of static.

"I can't believe this," Raina burst out. "It speaks the common language of interstellar space."

"Oh, Raina, you're so smart, you're stupid," Heck said. "A lot of this is *modern* technology. Of course, it would speak Interstellar."

Raina felt her face turn red. Then she poked at Heck's chest with her index finger. "Listen, Mr. Get-into-Trouble-All-the-Time Jordan, you find for me a single data chip in all of Galactic Command's data banks that explains this." She pointed at the human looking robot with her other index finger. "How can you explain a robot, no bigger that your hand, that completely changes its elemental properties and enlarges itself to over five feet tall?"

Heck was silenced. Maybe Raina's anger was as unnerving to him as the robot they were watching.

The robot took one step closer.

Ringo yelled, "Wait, we're on a rescue mission! Don't shoot us!"

There was a whirring as the robot's computer mind processed this information. Immediately it asked, "You are on a rescue mission?" The robot's speech pattern became clearer with every syllable.

"Yes, we are," Dai responded sincerely. "We're here to rescue the space pilot in this capsule."

The weapon disappeared back into the robot's arm. "Please stand away from the pod."

Dai directed them all to the wall on their right.

The robot, moving stiffly and making slight creaking and grinding noises, walked back to the panel above his small door. It examined the readouts on the panel's metallic face. Its hand depressed three control switches. An orifice on the panel emitted a series of brightly colored laser lights straight into the robot's eye lenses.

"I think it's communicating with the pod's computer system," Ringo suggested.

While the Rangers held their breath, the robot appeared to be processing information. Then it turned to face them. "Please remain where you are."

"Why would we want to do that?" Heck asked.

The robot's internal mechanisms started processing very loudly.

"That doesn't sound good," Dai muttered. "Heck, be careful."

"It's not good. It'll kill us in a minute," Raina answered. "Don't make it mad, Heck."

"What can we do?" Dai said, looking around helplessly.

The robot turned back toward the pod.

"What are you doing?" Heck called after it.

In its metallic, artificial voice, the robot said, "I am contacting Throsis. A rescue ship is on its way."

"But this escape pod has been adrift for thousands of years," Raina said. "There's no one left on Throsis!"

The robot stood absolutely still but finally said, "I cannot process your information. There is definitely a Throsis rescue ship on its way." The whirring sounds continued, and the robot said, "The main power relays were shut down, but power has been restored to the pod."

"I expect," Ringo said slowly, "the main computer matrix was protected and reprogrammed at the subsystems. Maybe you could interface with the main computer to get the subsystems back in order."

"I will attempt the maneuver," the robot said. "Stay back." The robot began manipulating the pod's external controls.

While the metal man did this, Raina watched Dai drift over to the *Daystar*'s portal and look out at the nebula they were approaching. The Ring Nebula appeared much larger now.

"I'm telling you"—Ringo's voice was trembling—"that robot's unnerving. It's unlike any technology we have."

"Well, he doesn't scare me," Heck bragged. "If you need any help, Raina, I'm right here."

Raina looked at him with exasperation. She well knew that he himself was frightened half to death by the talking robot, but he always had to cover up his shortcomings by boasting. "I don't need help," she told him. Secretly she was thinking, *And if I needed help, I'd want Dai to help me.*

She felt sure all four of them were frightened half to death. They were facing a situation beyond their abilities. Neither their science nor Dai's strength could save them. She said, "It's going to take the Lord to get us out of this."

While he was looking out the portal, Dai secretly drew his com link out of his uniform pocket. "Dai Bando to Captain Edge." The device failed to work.

Captain Edge strode down the main corridor of the *Daystar* toward the bridge. The amidships safety door was closed, and he pushed the switch. The door opened like a camera iris, and Edge stepped through it. He did not get far, however.

A dark, heavy shape struck him in the chest, and he fell backward to the deck.

"Contessa . . . get . . . off . . . me!" The dog and the captain rolled over each other on the main corridor. Clearly, the German shepherd thought it was all play, and she barked excitedly.

Edge sat up. "I see you're finally getting better." He rubbed her ears.

"*Woof.*" Contessa's deep voice filled the passageway.

By the time Jerusha hurriedly appeared with a worried look on her face, the captain was petting the dog on her head with one hand while rubbing her back with the other.

Contessa tried to lick his face. She loved attention, especially Captain Edge's attention.

Edge looked up and smiled at the dog's startled mistress. "Jerusha, I fought this dog as long as I could. She loves me so much that I've got to return the love a little."

He got to his feet. "Well, I guess I'm not too old to learn to love dogs—especially a dog that saved my life."

Jerusha acted relieved. "I thought you'd still be mad at me—for the way I acted back on the bridge."

"Not at all, Jerusha."

"I really was wrong, Captain. I'm sorry."

"We'll forget it." Edge put a hand on her shoulder. "We all make mistakes, and I've made more than my share. I've got a temper, and you have, too. That means both of us will have to work on it."

"Llewellen to Captain Edge. Llewellen to Captain Edge."

"Captain Edge here. What is it, Bronwen?"

"You'd better come to the bridge. Right away."

"Come on, Jerusha. Something's up." Edge grabbed her arm, and they raced down the corridor.

On the bridge, Zeno Thrax said urgently, "Over here, Captain."

"What is it, Zeno?"

"The scanners detect a large ship headed toward us."

"It's the *Pegasus.* Commandant Lee is scheduled to meet us here." Edge pointed to a spot on the viewer.

Thrax was pensive. "No, I don't believe that this is the *Pegasus*, Captain."

"Talk to me, First!"

"For one thing, this ship is heading toward us from an opposite sector of space from the *Pegasus.* Next, the ship is much larger than a Magnum Deep Space Cruiser. I've never seen a configuration like this."

"Where is it coming from?"

"I surmise it's from the planet Throsis."

"I thought there was nobody alive on Throsis! How could a ship be coming from there?"

"I don't know, sir, but there it is." Thrax turned to him and drew his lips together tightly. "Look at the size of it—maybe twice the size of a Magnum Space Cruiser. I've never seen anything like it."

Stepping closer to the screen, Captain Edge narrowed his eyes. "See if you can bring it up closer," he muttered.

Zeno adjusted the scanners.

The captain's jaw dropped, and he exclaimed, "What *is* that!"

Edge had been expecting to see a typical star cruiser. What he actually saw sent terror through him. The monster spaceship was painted deep red. It had a relief of colossal anacondas affixed to the hull. He couldn't count the number of weapons that protruded from it. "First, look at that armament array! A giant ship like this would have been designed for only one purpose—conquest!"

Everyone on the bridge drew in their breath.

"I've never seen anything like that either, Captain," Bronwen said softly.

For a time, the horror of the thing silenced them all, and they just watched as the monstrous spacecraft rocketed toward them.

Then, “What else could go wrong, Captain?” Thrax asked bleakly.

11
The Kidnapping

The silver robot stood motionless, but it blocked any access to the pod's external computer controls. Its highly polished silver skin made Raina think of mercury. Something about the mechanical man suddenly turned her legs to mush.

It had done nothing more than seem life threatening. In fact, it now appeared to be in its standby mode. After a while Heck dared to walk up to the quiet robot and lay a finger on its metallic shoulder.

"Heck, let it alone!"

"The robot looks like liquid metal," Heck reported, "but it's actually solid." He prodded a few other places. "I watched it bend its waist a while ago, though. Somehow this thing can bend without joints. It's incredible." Then he even pushed against the metal man. "It's like it's glued to the floor. I can't get it to move an inch."

"We're changing course," Raina said suddenly.

"I can tell. It feels like the ship is turning," Dai said.

The secondary navigation console was located in the cargo bay, and Raina sidled toward it. "*Daystar*'s changing course, all right," she said after a look at the data. "We'll skirt the nebula, but our new heading is taking us toward Sulaphat. What's going on?"

As the robot continued to stand motionless, Dai, Ringo, and Heck joined her. Heck adjusted the three control switches that focused the long-range scanner. The sensor alarms sounded, and the computer-enhanced image of a very large vessel appeared on the viewer.

Heck was the first to find words. "Look at the size of that ship! It's twice the size of any ship in Galactic Command."

Raina just stood still and said nothing. But she feared that something was going terribly wrong.

Dai asked, "What's wrong, Raina?"

"I just wish I knew what our mechanical friend over there meant by the word 'rescue'."

Ringo looked at her questioningly. "What are you thinking?"

Raina pointed to the giant spacecraft on the viewer. "I'm thinking that's the biggest ship I've ever seen." She scanned the ship's energy patterns. "More to the point—it's the biggest *warship* I've ever seen!" She turned to Dai Bando helplessly.

Dai kept his composure. "We have few choices, Raina. I guess right now we'll just have to wait and see what happens."

Ringo was watching the unmoving robot again. "Raina, try to change our heading slightly," he suggested. "See if we have helm control."

Raina adjusted the helm switches. They immediately returned to their original settings toward Sulaphat.

"Just as I thought." Ringo's voice was confident. "We thought the robot was interfacing with the pod computer, when it was really communicating with our navigation computer. It's controlling all the helm functions. We've got to do something."

Heck interjected, "We have to stop the ship, or maybe reverse our heading."

"If we can just move the robot, maybe then we can manipulate the pod's external controls and regain helm control," Ringo said.

Dai, Heck, and Ringo used all their strength to lift the inactive robot off the deck, but not even Dai's exceptional strength could move the mechanical man.

"This stupid piece of metal!" Heck yelled. He kicked the robot's leg. Of course, the robot didn't budge.

"Let's try again," Ringo said.

Again, the boys huffed and puffed and exerted all their strength, but still the mechanical man didn't budge a centimeter.

"All of you, stand back."

The three boys turned toward Raina.

She began concentrating very hard on the robot. An intense frown was set on her face.

"I keep forgetting she has that *implant*," Heck said.

When Raina was a small child, her parents were missionaries to a savage planet called Zacor. The Zacorians were little more than dangerous brute savages. Zacor was also home to many dangerous creatures. In order to protect their only daughter, her parents had a group of intergalactic scientists surgically implant a kinesthetic enhancer in Raina's brain. This device gave her the power to move things by her mind, when necessary. The implant frightened her, for it was a very powerful device. Using it drained her strength, also. Indeed, she always tried her best never to use it unless absolutely necessary.

"This robot's a lot bigger and heavier than a purple rat, Raina," Ringo said doubtfully.

Raina was concentrating too hard to answer. Controlling the brain wave enhancer took all her effort.

And then the robot began to shiver. The shiver turned into shaking. After a few moments, the robot started rising into the air, its mechanical body still standing straight. Now the cargo bay was completely lit up by the multicolored light patterns emitted from its metal skin.

"I don't think it's happy," Ringo said a little fearfully.

"Be careful," Dai said to Raina. He looked ready to throw himself headlong onto the robot if anything dangerous were to happen.

Steadily, Raina's concentration moved the gleaming silver robot to the back of the cargo bay. When she gently set it down on the deck, its sea of flashing lights calmed back to normal.

"Set it on its side, can you?" Dai suggested. "Then, if it wants to move, maybe it will have a harder time getting to its feet."

Very gingerly, Raina turned the robot onto its right side.

Dai had just begun to congratulate Raina when she began to fall. As usual, this ordeal had drained her. Dai caught her in a split second.

"I just need to . . . rest for a moment," Raina said softly.

Dai looked around the cargo bay for a place to put her down.

A small smile appeared on Raina's lips. "You can just hold me for a while, if you like."

"I think it would be best if I sat you down on the deck."

"Over here against the bulkhead," Ringo told him. "She'll never relax if she's anywhere close to that robot."

Dai set Raina down against the wall opposite the mechanical man.

"Ringo, stop fussing over Her Majesty and get yourself over here!" Heck whined.

Raina could see that Heck was trying to figure out the pod controls. He was flipping switches as fast as he could.

"We've got only minutes before that ship gets here!" he yelled.

Ringo rushed to Heck's side.

"We're not going to make it!" Heck screamed. "The helm won't respond, and we don't have time to take this computer apart."

Dai was still bending over Raina and trying to make her comfortable. Suddenly, she cried out and gripped his arm. "Look out the portal!"

Everyone had been so preoccupied with moving the robot and trying to get helm control that no one had paid attention to the giant ship. It was now upon them. The red color of the warship's hull filled the portal.

"It's got snakes on it!" Heck yelled in fear. "They're huge. I hate snakes."

Raina saw the snakes and realized that they were painted on. But they were indeed "huge."

The warship flew in a graceful arc and came up behind *Daystar.* A large door was located on the lower portion of its bow. This apparently was the warship's hanger door. Even the door was in the shape of an anaconda's head.

Raina could tell that the power systems aboard *Daystar* were being shut down one by one. Only the faint emergency lights remained working in the cargo bay.

"Ayee!"

A bloodcurdling mechanical shriek filled the cargo bay. The robot was on its feet. Its multicolored lights swirled in patterns too fast for the human eye to follow. Its scanner eyes were twin beams of light that resembled lasers.

Heck rubbed his eyes and screamed over and over, "I'm blind! I'm blind!"

Dai yelled, "Don't look at it! Nobody look at it!"

Raina turned her back to the robot and made sure she stayed that way.

As the warship closed in on *Daystar*, the anaconda-head doors opened, revealing a large hanger deck. Dark orange light shone from the anaconda's eyes, bathing Captain Edge's ship. *Daystar* was jolted for a moment, and then its engines completely shut down.

"It's a tractor beam," Ringo and Heck said simultaneously.

In minutes, the dark orange beams had pulled the *Daystar* into the warship's hanger bay, and its huge doors shut tight.

On the bridge, the *Daystar* crew stood in silence and astonishment. They had just witnessed the ingestion of their cruiser by the giant spaceship. Every effort to rescue themselves had been futile. The main computer control seemed to have a mind of its own.

Captain Edge felt the warship roar away with engines that probably were larger than *Daystar* herself. "Bronwen, where's it headed?"

"Definitely headed for Sulaphat, Captain. And Throsis is the only inhabitable planet in its system."

Edge shook himself back to reality and blinked as if to clear his vision. He had never seen such a thing as this in all his life, nor had he even heard of such a thing. "Check all systems. Let's see how bad we are," he commanded Zeno.

"Aye, sir," Zeno Thrax said and started the systems checks. "I've seen starships decorated with birds of prey, creatures of the sea, and just about every four-legged predator you can imagine," he said, "but I've never seen one that was covered with giant snakes.

This is something I would not have believed if someone had told me."

"Nor would I," Edge responded.

Bronwen was able to make a few calculations, and then she looked up at the captain. "We should arrive at Throsis in a couple of hours."

Edge chewed his lower lip. "It appears that our less critical systems are still functional. Zeno, stop what you're doing and see if you can give me a quick readout on the planet Throsis."

Zeno rapidly did his work on the instruments in front of him. "Sir, the land masses of Throsis are almost completely dominated by swamps."

"The planet is one big swamp?"

"No, but it appears that the swampy areas are interconnected. So indeed the planet is *mostly* swamp."

"What else is it?"

"Well, the planet has one supersized volcano. Right here, sir. You see? It's located on the equatorial belt."

"Yes, I see it. Anything special about it?"

"The volcano seems to be dormant, but deep space beacons have picked up some power emissions in the recent past." Thrax scrolled through the data. "The energy modulations aren't being produced by nature."

That sounded like trouble to Captain Edge. "What's your best guess, First?"

"I truly don't know, Captain. I've never encountered readings like this."

At the edge of the Ring Nebula, Sir Richard Irons and Francesca Del Ray watched the gobbling up of the *Daystar*.

"Captain," he ordered, "pull us back into the nebula."

"Aye, sir." The captain of the *Jackray* issued the appropriate commands.

The orders were obeyed, though moving back into the Ring Nebula was dangerous. Irons knew that the men who worked for him had little use for standards. What kept them in line was fear, and he'd always known how to use fear in controlling his men—with the exception of Mark Edge. Somehow Edge had slipped away from him. It was a betrayal that Sir Richard Irons would make right someday.

"What's your plan now?" Francesca Del Ray's question sounded more like an accusation. *She* knew he had not planned on the appearance of the gigantic warship, and he knew that she knew.

"My plan is to do what I always do—improvise," he replied curtly.

"In other words, you don't have the slightest idea, do you?" Her tone was scornful.

"Someday you're going to push me too far," he said angrily.

Cold daggers shot from Francesca's ice-blue eyes. "I'll push you as far as I like."

She had dared to belittle him in front of the whole bridge crew. Irons said fiercely, "Never forget this, my dear"—rage oozed from his every syllable—"an ancient philosopher once said, 'Don't live as if you had a thousand years ahead of you. Death is soaring over your head, so as long as you live, as long as you really can, be good.'" His eyes locked with hers. "That means be good to *me*."

Francesca's "daggers" were no match for Sir Richard Irons's "broadsword," and she was silent.

The whole bridge crew stood frozen where they were standing. Clearly, their master had shown his strength in a way that turned their backbones to jelly.

"Snap out of it," Sir Richard commanded loudly. Then he turned to the captain. "Captain, follow the warship, but stay out of sensor range." Captain and crew rushed to comply with his orders.

Then Irons angrily headed for the bridge elevator, motioning for Francesca to follow him. "Come with me. I have something to say to you in private."

The elevator door closed upon them. And as it did, Francesca Del Ray began to realize that she had given her loyalty to someone as evil as the Dark One himself. For the first time in her life, she silently cried to God for help.

12
The Robot Colony

Inside the *Daystar*'s cargo bay, the Space Rangers stood in silent submission to the silver robot. Its scanner eyes were trained on them. But the laserlike light had faded from its lenses, and the pattern and speed of lights that effused from its metallic skin had slowed considerably. The robot nodded its mechanical head in the direction of the main hatch, and the door mechanism engaged.

"He had control of *Daystar* the whole time," Ringo murmured.

"He must have some sort of internal transmitter that communicates with the main computer," Raina added.

Dai was looking through *Daystar*'s cargo bay portal. "I think we better do as it says. Look out there." He pointed.

The warship's hanger bay was occupied by many robots that looked exactly like the one that had been aboard the pod.

One by one, each Space Ranger exited from the *Daystar* until they all stood together on the warship's hanger deck, surrounded by sleek, silver-colored robots.

Their guard returned its weapon to the storage compartment on its arm and at once looked like every other robot.

For a few moments, the Rangers looked nervously at the mechanical people and then at each other. At last Raina broke the silence. "Who *are* you?" she asked cautiously.

One robot, which had no markings that would distinguish it from the others, took two steps forward.

"Is that the one that was on the escape pod?" Heck spoke as if his throat was filled with sawdust. "I can't tell."

"Who knows? Every robot looks exactly the same," replied Ringo.

The robot took another step toward them, then stopped. Its color patterns increased a little. "You must come with us." It motioned the Rangers to the rear of the hanger area.

"What about Galan Knowles?" Dai asked.

The robot spoke in mechanical precision. "Galan Knowles will be rejuvenated."

A robot guard led Captain Edge, Jerusha Ericson, Bronwen Llewellen, Zeno Thrax, and Ivan Petroski into the warship's hangar bay. The captain immediately saw a troubled looking group of Space Rangers—Raina, Ringo, Heck. Where Studs Cagney and the grunts were, no one indicated.

"We don't understand," Edge asked Raina softly. "What's going on?"

The robot led them all into an area that must have once functioned as quarters for the now extinct human crew. Immediately the escape pod was also brought in.

"I am the robot who was on board your ship," the robot said. It then directed the *Daystar* crew to a table located in the center of the main day room.

When they were seated, the robot said, "My name is Primal One, and I am the leader of the robot colony on Throsis. Do not fear for your other crew members. They are safe and are being cared for."

Edge was astonished when several identical

robots brought in plates of fruit along with cups and several pitchers of fruit punch and placed them on the table. Primal One indicated that the humans should help themselves. These robot people were treating them as guests rather than as prisoners. What, indeed, was going on?

"Our story is long, and we do not have much time. There are two ships pursuing us. We must speedily get back to protect our base. Our spacecraft is our colony's primary defense."

A giant viewer dropped from the ceiling. It showed the panorama of the entire Lyra Sector. Primal One indicated each ship's position, heading, and speed.

"Galan Knowles," Primal One told them, "rescued me after my ship crashed on Earth's moon. After he had repaired my computer matrix, I explained to him that I was searching for the home planet of the wise race that had created us.

"Galan Knowles informed me that our creators, the Amesstorites, had become extinct due to a catastrophe of unknown origin."

"But how did the two of you come to be on an escape pod together, floating in space?" Ringo asked.

"Galan Knowles had powerful enemies, though I saw him perform only great works of kindness. Mankind is still a puzzle to us. Sometimes you destroy the good and applaud the evil." The robot's speech patterns became smoother. "My ship was beyond repair, so Galan Knowles agreed to pilot an Explorer ship to the Lyra Sector. He felt that he had an obligation to take me back to Throsis. He stated that the uniqueness of my metallurgy was too tempting for Earth's scientists—and for his personal enemies. I would wind up disassembled and pieced out to firms all over Earth.

"On the way to Throsis, I used the knowledge my

wise creators planted in me to modify the Explorer's escape pod in case it should be needed. That was fortunate, since Sheliak had a radiation burst that sped toward our craft. With only minutes to spare, Galan Knowles and I marooned ourselves aboard the escape pod. I reduced my size and energy needs, occasionally taking a space walk to collect neutron emissions. Galan Knowles remained frozen in cryogenic sleep."

"For five thousand years," Jerusha murmured.

"Galan Knowles was in cryogenic freeze. So he will have no memory of time passed. And we robots don't measure time the way a human does. It's hard to explain, but for us a half second can seem like years, and five thousand years can seem like a second."

Edge felt mind boggled. The *Daystar* humans had no way to understand this concept. Humans were time bound. Their lives were marked by the passage of time.

The robot walked over to the portal and seemed to look out into space.

Thrax asked courteously, "This may sound like a strange question, but are you a sentient being?"

The robot continued to face the stars. "Our highly intelligent creators designed us with advanced artificial intelligence. We are capable of performing many tasks and can act on our own initiative within set parameters. Electronically, our brains function similarly to yours. Although there are differences between us, our thought patterns are similar to yours. We cannot procreate like humans, but we do propagate ourselves through the manufacturing of other robots. Our experiences and knowledge are transferred into the new robots' memory core. Just as humans learn, we learn. Just as humans embrace life, we embrace being operational. For us robots, being operational *is* life." The robot stopped speaking.

"Then, *are* you a sentient being?" Zeno Thrax repeated.

The robot processed for a moment and then answered. "Our creators, the Amesstorites, instructed us that only the Father of the Heavens can create sentient beings. We are not the creation of God. We are the creation of man. Thus, we are not sentient. If we fail to re-energize, we stop operating. We do not possess an eternal mind like the human mind, which remains cognitive even after the brain has been destroyed."

The robot's manners and responses were profound. It was no wonder, the captain thought, that Galan Knowles believed Primal One was worth saving.

"I have a question," Heck said suddenly and earnestly. "It's been bugging me since I pushed that green button during our space walk."

The robot's expression was always changeless. It gave Captain Edge absolutely no clue as to its abilities or communicative skills or pleasure or displeasure.

Heck took a big bite from a fruit whose taste resembled that of an apple and a tangerine. "This is delicious."

Dai frowned at him. "*What* question, Heck? Primal One is waiting. Can't you stop eating for a while until we sort things out?"

"Sure." Heck stuffed a few pieces of fruit into his tool bag.

Dai took a deep breath and exhaled slowly. "What is your question?"

"The cryogenic freeze," Heck began. "Frozen human cells turn to crystals, thus making it impossible to rejuvenate someone in cryogenic sleep."

"Our creators, the Amesstorites, were aware of this. With their great wisdom they developed a means of overcoming that problem."

"How did they *do* that?" Heck asked, very curious.

"We robots have a biochemical fluid that runs through our bodies much the same as blood circulates through yours," the robot continued. "At my direction—before he was placed in cryogenic sleep—Galan Knowles transfused some of my fluid into his bloodstream."

"Wow!" Heck exclaimed. "Cryogenic antifreeze. So Galan Knowles's cells were prevented from crystalizing."

Captain Edge had been silent all this time, watching and listening and learning. But something was troubling him. Where were Temple Cole and Mei-Lani Lao?

"Primal One, I see that two of our women are not here . . ." he began.

"They are still aboard your craft. One is not well? They are safe."

Edge took out his com link. "May I?" he asked. Then, "Edge to sick bay."

"Sick bay here, Captain," Temple Cole responded. "What is going on?"

"We've experienced some systems shutdown. What's sick bay's energy status?"

"Sick bay is fully operational. There has been no energy reduction here," the ship's surgeon told him.

"How's your patient?"

"She's stable for now," Temple Cole said. "That dust that Mei-Lani inhaled—the computer banks were finally able to isolate it as the cause of her sickness."

"Dust? What dust?"

"Dust from Deneb."

"How could that happen?" Edge was getting very tired of more surprises.

"You remember the giant statue of Shiva that you approved for the training area?" Cole asked gently.

"Of course, I remember it. Did it have Deneb dust on it?"

"From what Tara Jaleel has told me, the statue is an ancient artifact that was crafted on Deneb. All the materials used in its construction were from Deneb. When the statue exploded . . ."

"Wait a minute—the statue exploded?" Edge interrupted as he tried to process all this.

"Tara doesn't know how it happened, but the statue exploded. It turned into a pile of dust. The explosion also sent a huge cloud of dust particles into the corridor. Mei-Lani just happened to be in the corridor at the time. Before she knew what was happening, she'd breathed in a large quantity of the dust. Something in the dust is poisoning her. I'm working on chemical analysis at this time."

"Who knows what the properties of Deneb soil are? That area of space has been bombarded with radiation for thousands of years!"

"Jaleel brought me some of the dust for analysis. I might as well have asked her for her foot. She respects the dust more than she respects herself. If Mei-Lani's life weren't at stake, Tara would never have given it to me."

"Captain Edge," the robot interrupted. "Please come now to our bridge. I'm certain you would like to watch our approach to Throsis. It is an exhilarating experience —even for us."

"Dr. Cole, I'll keep in contact. Edge out."

Fascinated, Captain Edge monitored the main viewer on the bridge of the warship. "Zeno, Throsis is just as you said—a planet dominated by swamps."

Huge areas looked similar to the Asian countries of Earth when they were flooded during monsoon season. There appeared to be water everywhere with only trees to climb to dry off.

"This world has many exotic and dangerous life-forms," the robot informed them. "Be warned and do not travel off without escort. Some of the animals are very large and would consider you a food source."

Heck interjected excitedly, "Those swamps are as big as continents—with oceans separating them, just like on Earth. And look at the color of the oceans!"

The dark blue seas contrasted beautifully with the brilliant green-and-brown colors of the swamps. Due to the dual stars of Sulaphet, there were no north or south polar regions. Throsis was brilliantly lit up during the day, but the planet had only twilight at night. Several moons were still visible during the daytime, giving the scene a surreal look.

"It's truly beautiful," Raina said. "But where did the Amesstorite people live—in the trees?"

The robot turned to Raina. "No, our intelligent creators lived where we live now—within the volcano. The interior of the planet has many dry caverns to live in. There are naturally occurring geothermal hot springs as well as mineral-rich springwater."

"A health nut's heaven," Heck said thoughtfully. "Say, do you guys have candy bars?"

"If you will give us the preparation instructions, I shall see that you are furnished with all the 'candy bars' you require," the robot answered.

Every human being on the bridge turned to Heck.

The captain voiced what everybody else surely was thinking. "No way, Heck. You've had enough candy bars. It's getting to where the Star Drive engines are not able to handle all the weight you've put on."

Heck fumed but remained silent.

And now the warship was approaching the volcano.

"The only appreciable land mass on the planet is this gigantic volcano," Bronwen murmured, as the ship drew near the thirty-thousand-feet-high mass of cold lava. "The volcano is definitely inactive. Readings on their sensors reveal that the base of the volcano is connected to a series of tunnels that transverse the entire planet." She scrolled the viewer. "Some of the tunnels open into huge caverns. They are too symmetrical to be natural caverns. They've been built by highly intelligent engineers."

The warship descended into the volcano's gaping mouth. The interior walls of the volcanic mountain began rushing by the portals. It was a precarious movement and could have ended in disaster, but Primal One performed masterfully at the controls. Finally the ship came to a halt at the interior base of the volcano. At once, Edge saw more robots, looking exactly like Primal One, approach the spacecraft and go about their duties in Throsis's only spaceport.

Standing at the portal, Heck said in wonder, "Would you look at that? Some of the large robots, like Primal One here, have just changed into little robots. You know—like Primal One was when we first saw him."

Several of the tiny robots entered through a miniature door.

"The smaller size is oftentimes more effective for maintenance operations," Primal One said. "Our creators were wise."

Edge leaned back and expelled his breath slowly. "That was one exciting experience, First." Then he smiled at his first officer. "I must say it was my first time to rocket down into the bowels of a volcano."

Zeno Thrax cleared his throat and seemed to agree. "I don't think there's another star fleet captain in the galaxy who could have brought this ship in as Primal One just did. Not even you, sir."

Such complimentary words were rare from Zeno Thrax, and Edge looked at him in surprise. "Do you truly mean that, Zeno?"

"Why, sir, I always mean what I say."

"You do, don't you?" Then Edge turned to the portal and let his gaze wander over their new surroundings. An enormous pit gaped just to the left of the spaceship. "And I'd hate to fall into *that,*" he mused.

"Look at that, sir. There are snakes at the bottom of that pit. Enormous snakes!" Zeno Thrax said. "They must be at least a hundred feet long and twelve feet around."

Edge looked down and narrowed his eyes. "Awful looking things."

Bronwen and the Rangers crowded close to the portal to have a look.

Primal One explained what they saw. "When our intelligent creators perished thousands of years ago, they left their computers and robotics operational. Thus we have retained their great knowledge. Many Earthmen have tried to colonize the planet and discover that knowledge, but the creatures that inhabit the swamps are too many and too formidable."

"What are these creatures in the pit?" Bronwen asked.

The robot responded, "These 'snakes' that you see are but anacond-droids, not true reptiles. They were created to protect and serve the Amesstorites. They are also able to traverse long, vertical tunnels better than conventional transports."

Even as the robot finished speaking, one of the anacond-droids raised its head over the lip of the pit and opened its mouth wide. At once, several silver robots began to carry boxes into the mechanical snake.

"I wouldn't want to meet one of them out in the swamps," Ringo said with a grimace on his face.

"The droids would not harm humankind—unless, of course, you were a clear and present danger to one of us. Otherwise, they are harmless and perform their duties in a satisfactory manner," Primal One explained. "But the swamps do have a variety of large organic anacondas. Some of these find their way into the tunnels and could swallow a human very quickly. Please do not travel anywhere on Throsis without a robot escort. Some of the planet's animal and aquatic life-forms are lethal."

"I'd like to bag a few of those swamp snakes." Heck seemed to envision himself as a big game hunter. "The only good snake is a dead snake."

"Heck," Captain Edge joked warmly, clapping a hand on his shoulder, "the snakes probably feel the same way about you."

13

The Cryogenic Capsule

Primal One walked slowly toward the *Daystar* captain. "A general broadcast alert is being scanned by our computers," it announced. Then the robot hesitated, as though puzzled. "Captain Edge, someone by the name of Commandant Lee is requesting communication with you . . ."

"That is my superior officer. Is there a place where I can speak with her in private?" Edge inquired.

The robot pointed toward a console. "That terminal has been secured for you."

Then Primal One and the other robots walked away from the communications area, leaving only *Daystar*'s officers and the Rangers with Captain Edge. In a few seconds, Commandant Lee's face appeared on the viewer.

"Captain, where *are* you? We reached the rendezvous point an hour ago." The commandant's face looked strained, and her forehead was deeply furrowed.

"We are inside a gigantic volcano at a robot base camp on the planet Throsis."

"I won't ask how you got there," Lee said with a sigh. "What is your status?"

"Except for Mei-Lani, we are fine. She's still fighting some strange illness. But the robots are very friendly and interesting. They seem to have been given all the advanced knowledge that their manufacturers possessed. They—or their inventors—have built the largest warship I've ever seen, and apparently it's just for defense. It appears to be three times the size of *Pegasus*. Anyway, they brought us here—they thought they were rescuing us. But we're safe."

"Robots . . . well . . ." She sighed again. "I do have in my possession some information on an extraordinary robot designated Primal One," Lee stated thoughtfully. "It seems that it had exceptional artificial intelligence, and records indicate that Galan Knowles was somehow involved with its crash on the moon."

"Commandant, we've learned that the reason Galan Knowles went into deep space was to return Primal One to his home—Throsis."

Captain Edge told her what he knew. "Primal One is the leader of this robot colony. He—or it—and all the rest of the robot population have treated us with great respect and consideration."

Just then Captain Pursey appeared on the viewer and interrupted their conversation. The commandant listened while he briefed her on some presumably new development. After some moments, she returned to Edge.

"The robot's warship probably did rescue you, Mark."

"How? We didn't need rescuing." He was confused.

"Our sensors have just detected an interstellar stealth signature orbiting Throsis. We are fairly certain it is the *Jackray*."

"Then Irons must have followed us here from the Ring Nebula!"

"The Ring Nebula—that gives me an idea. Is *Daystar* functional?" Lee asked.

"We lost main computer control just before we

were tractored into the robot warship. I believe Primal One intends to restore main computer control to us shortly."

"Captain, get your ship ready for departure. *Pegasus* is about to engage the *Jackray*. Irons will realize that we can scan him, so he'll run. And the only place he'll have to run to is the Ring Nebula. We'll remain hot on his tail so that he'll fly into the nebula at full speed. It will be a long time before he finds his way out."

Thoughtfully, she looked past Edge into the room behind him. "Mark, as you know, our science still has not completely resolved the problem of resuscitating one who is in cryogenic sleep. So I will leave this next part completely to your discretion. My preference is for you to bring Galan Knowles back to Earth. But if, in your estimation, it seems better to leave him at the robot colony for the time being—then do so. But wait until we clear the Sulaphat system before you make your departure." Then she smiled around at the entire *Daystar* crew. "Lee out."

Primal One seemingly detected that the communication link had terminated, for he came back into the communications area.

"Commandant Lee is the leader of Galactic Command," Edge told him. "She has ordered us to depart Throsis. Her first thought was for us to take Galan Knowles back to Earth. However, Earth's science still—"

"Very well. We will immediately reverse the rejuvenation process that has been begun and will place Galan Knowles back into cryogenic sleep."

"But how do—"

"Our scanners indicate that your commandant's ship is pursuing another spacecraft toward the Ring Nebula—at high speed. Did you know this?"

That brought Captain Edge back to *Daystar*'s big

problem. "That is correct. The owner of that ship is Sir Richard Irons—a very evil man."

"I see," Primal One responded. "But once he speeds deep into the nebula, he will be lost a long time."

"Not long enough," Edge replied. "Irons will figure a way out. Maybe not immediately, but soon enough."

The robots began going over the *Daystar* with a fine-tooth comb. The larger robots performed maintenance and repair to the accessible areas of the ship, while the tiny robots performed similar jobs in the less accessible places. *Daystar*'s main computer control was returned to the bridge, and her fuel cells were replenished.

"Sir," Edge found himself saying to Primal One, then thought how foolish that sounded. But he had great respect for this amazing mechanical man. "Sir, I must tell you—Earth science has not quite learned how to resuscitate humans who are in cryogenic sleep . . ." He hesitated, hardly daring to ask.

But he did not have to ask. "Ah," the robot said. "It is a simple matter when the person has been properly inoculated, as Galan Knowles was. I shall give you a DNA rejuvenator. A remarkable electronic device. I shall also give you an electronic record of how our creators used it to treat other medical problems in this part of the galaxy."

Six robots, carrying Galan Knowles's escape pod, arrived at *Daystar*'s cargo bay. The space pilot was still in cryogenic sleep. They were about to set down the pod in the exact location where they had previously found it.

"Not there, please," Captain Edge called from across the cargo area. "Take the pod up to sick bay. Dr.

Cole will want to treat him there. Ringo, show them where to go."

The robots, carrying the pod and without missing a beat, followed Ringo out into the corridor and on toward sick bay. They soon were back and exiting the same way they had come.

Primal One walked into *Daystar*'s cargo bay then and located Captain Edge. "If you are ever in this sector again, we hope that you will stop for a visit," he said. As usual, the robot could not have been more congenial.

"You can count on it," Edge promised. "And thank you once more for the medical information. By the way, be careful. Commandant Lee says that Sir Richard's *Jackray* is deep inside the Ring Nebula. But be on the lookout for her. Irons has a way of showing up unexpectedly."

"He sounds like a gifted but evil man," Primal One replied.

"He is. And believe me, he can sweet-talk you. Just after you decide to trust him, he changes colors."

"Good-bye, Captain, and a pleasant voyage." Primal One debarked from *Daystar*.

"Edge to Thrax."

"Thrax here."

"Shut the hatches and get us out of here."

"Aye, sir."

The hatches closed, and the cruiser's thrusters maneuvered her out of the warship. Thrax turned her nose vertical, and they thundered up the interior wall of the volcano. After only a few moments, the blue skies of Throsis turned into the star-spangled night of outer space.

The *Daystar* was speeding back toward Earth. The escape pod was secured inside sick bay. The grunts were cleaning the biochemical fluid from the pod's exterior surface. They talked quietly about all that had happened. Temple Cole stood by watching and listening.

"Doesn't it seem like a miracle to you, Ivan," she said to the chief engineer, "that we actually have Galan Knowles in our sick bay?"

"Just a coincidence," Petroski said.

"You don't really believe that."

"Of course, I believe it. Coincidences happen all the time."

Temple turned to the small man and said gently, "Is that really all that's in your heart? Don't any of your people believe in God?"

Ivan Petroski suddenly lowered his head. He did not answer for a moment but stood twisting his hands together. "My mother did," he said finally.

"Ah ha!" Temple smiled. "And you loved your mother, didn't you?"

"Sure I did," Petroski said. "She was good to me."

"And you think she was a fool, then, for believing in God."

"Don't you say bad things about my mother!" Ivan snapped back.

"But if she believed in God and you don't, you must think that you know more than she did."

"I don't want to talk about it," Petroski said. "But don't you say anything bad about my mother."

Temple Cole sent up a silent prayer for Ivan Petroski. He had a gentle spot in him as far as his mother was concerned, and she prayed, *Lord, let this gentleness spread, that he may find a better way of life. That he may find You.*

Bronwen Llewellen also was standing by, waiting to get her first glimpse of Galan Knowles. She was probably glad to have someone on the ship who was older than she was—frozen or not!

Temple moved over beside her. "Bronwen, you know we have to be very careful."

"Yes, I know. It's a very delicate process."

"Galan Knowles may have tampered with the pod computers."

"That sounds like something he might do. He was always impulsive, according to all the reports."

Temple frowned. "I think he adjusted the command computers to operate on different parameters."

Both women stood gazing intently at the frozen face through the front glass of the capsule.

"He doesn't look five thousand years old, does he, Bronwen?"

"No, indeed!"

The face was that of a man about forty years old rather than five thousand. It was a ruggedly handsome face. The hair was thick and dark, with a touch of red in the brown. The features were strong and very masculine.

"I wonder," Temple asked quietly, "what his thoughts will be when he wakes up?" Then she said, "We are so blessed, Bronwen, to have access to the unbelievable medical know-how of the Amesstorites. Just think of it! Without their science, there was a good chance he would never survive his cryogenic sleep."

Bronwen smiled and said firmly, "And he will survive it. It would seem that God so wills. I pray that he does," she breathed softly. "There are so many questions that I want to ask him."

In the sick bay behind Dr. Cole, Ringo and Heck attached new computers and circuit pathways to the cryogenic capsule.

"Dr. Cole is loading us down with work again," Heck muttered softly. "Why doesn't she get the grunts to do this grunt work?"

"Stop complaining. You're supposed to be working on developing a positive attitude, remember," Ringo reminded him.

Heck's hands moved swiftly and capably, repairing circuit pathways. "I guess those robots just plain forgot to do any maintenance on the escape pod. But never fear—Heck is here!"

Ringo continued working and tried to ignore Heck's bragging.

"Did you see how I used my antigrav circuits to reactivate the pod's computer? Pretty smart, huh?" Heck gave a little bow and said loudly, "I guess that'll show everybody a thing or two."

Ringo shook his head in disgust. "Heck, there is no end to your self-centeredness. And all your bragging is really much ado about nothing."

"Well, it was my brains that allowed Dr. Cole to remove the safety features from the pod and place them into the sick bay's computer banks."

"Nobody's denying that," Ringo said.

The doctor seemed about to start the rejuvenation process. In her hand she held Primal One's device for resuscitation from cryogenic storage. She looked around and said, "You two—you're either going to have to be quiet or leave! Both of you!"

"What's that thing you've got, Dr. Cole?" Heck asked.

Before the doctor could respond, Ringo said, "It's a DNA rejuvenator. It directly restructures DNA ruptures into valid organic code. It does other stuff too. We got it from the robots."

Cole nodded in agreement, said, "Now, *shhh!*" and turned to the frozen body.

Both boys grew very quiet. After all, it was not every day that one got to see someone being reanimated from a cryogenic freeze.

Dr. Cole looked about at all her instruments and at the DNA rejuvenator, as though making sure there would be no mistakes. Sick bay was so still that Ringo could hear the humming of the processors. The faces of the instruments cast a green glow over the room.

Ringo was thinking, *What will a man be like who has slept for five thousand years?*

Galan Knowles's mind slowly and steadily drifted from the depths of oblivion to the warm, sunny heights of consciousness.

First, it seemed he was sitting in a beautiful green valley. Bright flowers were scattered through the grass, flowers of every color imaginable. He could smell their fragrance. He especially liked the lavender irises and the yellow daffodils.

"Do you remember the first time we met?"

He looked over at his wife. "I think about it every day, Gloria. God has been so good to me."

"He's been good to me too." She smiled.

Galan Knowles was a happy man. He had everything. "I still remember every word that I said in our marriage ceremony."

"Do you, Galan?"

"Yes. I promised to be faithful to you as long as I live, and I will be, too."

"That's sweet."

Then, suddenly it was winter. Instead of sitting with his wife in a beautiful valley, he was standing over her grave. Freezing rain was falling. The sight of the ugly, raw red earth of the grave struck him like a blow.

"Gloria," he whispered, "why did you have to leave me?"

There were no answers.

"I'm going away soon, Gloria. I'm going to participate in the Exploration Expeditions. I have to save a friend of mine named Primal One. If you hadn't left me, I never would go on such a dangerous mission. But now I don't really care. I'm headed for Throsis, and I don't know when I'll be back. Or if I will be." Cold rain soaked his clothing. It dripped down his collar, and it made a puddle at his feet. But he hardly noticed.

His vision shifted again, and abruptly he was in a warm place and Gloria was there again, an alive Gloria. He was looking into her face. "Everything will be all right," she was saying.

As he reached out to touch her, she began to fade away. "It was all a dream," he cried. "It was all a dream!"

But then he saw a bright light and a woman's face in front of him. It was not Gloria, for this woman had strawberry hair and violet eyes. He heard a voice say, "Dr. Cole, he's coming out of it." He felt the touch of hands. And then warmth flooded him. Somehow he knew that he had been on a long journey and had now arrived at home.

14
The Frozen Space Pilot

Francesca Del Ray tossed restlessly on the bed in her quarters, thinking. Sir Richard Irons was such an evil man. Never in her wildest dreams had she known that evil could be so dark. And she had foolishly flirted with evil, mocked it, even laughed at it. Evil was something she could control, she'd thought. Doing her own thing was the pathway to self-fulfillment, she'd thought. She did not think so anymore. Just minutes ago, she'd realized that doing her own thing could cost her her life.

Her mother had once told her, "Francesca, if you live for the devil, the devil will have his due."

Francesca, of course, had laughed at that. Reaping what you sow might apply to some people, but Francesca never thought that meant her.

She continued thinking. She had never seen Sir Richard so angry with her. She had heard evil in his threats. She had seen evil on his face. It had been a face filled with rage and hatred. It was the evil in that face that now focused her thought on escape.

Even now she could hear Irons yelling angrily at the captain out in the corridor. "Get us out of here at once!"

"I can't change the laws of physics!" the captain of the *Jackray* protested. "This ship is deep inside the Ring Nebula—perhaps light years inside. We can't just fly her out. Our scanners are inoperative."

"Then repair them! I demand that you do something about this. I'm not going to spin my wheels and waste my time floating around this nebula."

"Sir Richard," the captain said, "our electronics people are working on the problem. They have a theory about charting our position with engine wakes. It's never been tried, but the theory is solid. If we can design and implement the right circuitry, we may be able to backtrack our engine wake to our point of entry."

"Well, make the necessary changes fast and contact me immediately when you have finished the linkups."

"Aye, sir." The captain apparently went off to do Sir Richard's bidding.

The patient was lying on his back. Bronwen Llewellen stood on one side of him and Dr. Cole on the other. For a long time the only sound was the harsh rasping of Galan Knowles's heavy breathing. Then he began to move his head slowly.

Finally he muttered, "Where did she go? I need Gloria."

The doctor murmured, "He's almost out of it now. Most likely he has been experiencing memories that are very real to him."

As Bronwen leaned forward, studying his face, Galan Knowles suddenly opened his eyes. They darted back and forth. There was panic in them and confusion.

"Everything will be all right. Don't be afraid," Bronwen said comfortingly.

"Is it you, Gloria?" His vision still appeared to be blurred.

She squeezed his hand. "No, my name is Bronwen."

The space pilot stiffened, and his eyes opened wide. "Who are you?"

"You must be very brave, Galan."

"Who are you?" he whispered. "You're not Gloria."

"My name is Bronwen Llewellen," she said gently but firmly. "Galan, how much do you remember?"

He frowned, thinking. "The escape pod . . . I was going to put myself . . . into a long sleep . . ."

"That's right. And that's what you did. You've been asleep a very long time, Galan."

The space pilot looked up at her, then at Dr. Cole. "How—how long?" he asked. "How long have I been asleep?"

"Five thousand years," Bronwen said quietly. She thought the truth would be best, and she knew of no way to soften the news.

At first he seemed not to know what to do with this new information. Confusion swept over his face.

"I—I was talking to Gloria," he whispered. "Just now."

Dr. Cole leaned toward him. "I think that probably you were, but it was in a dream. We often think of the things we love best when we are just coming awake."

Knowles swept the sick bay with his gaze. "Where am I?" he asked.

Temple Cole said, "You're aboard the space cruiser *Daystar*. I'm the ship's medical officer."

He groaned. "Where are we? Where are you going? Where are you taking me?"

"Back to Earth."

"There's nothing for me back on Earth. Don't take me there," he begged.

Bronwen exchanged glances with Dr. Cole, but there was nothing they could do. Now that the space pilot was resuscitated, Commandant Lee would certainly want him returned to Earth as soon as possible.

"And where's Primal One?"

Dr. Cole explained that Primal One was back on

Throsis. “You are awake because of Primal One and the Amesstorites’ DNA rejuvenator. Our commandant wants us to return you to Earth with us.”

For some time the man lay quietly.

Then Ringo Smith came close to adjust the computer located near the head of Galan Knowles’s bed. As he leaned down to do so, the medallion he always wore about his neck fell out of his shirt.

Knowles startled. “Where did you get that?” he gasped.

Ringo looked startled himself at being spoken to. “It was a family heirloom, sir,” he said. “I’ve worn it almost since I was a baby.”

Bronwen Llewellen could see that Knowles was upset.

“What’s the name of your family?” he asked.

“I’ve always been called Ringo Smith, sir,” he said. “But I found out not long ago that my family name is really Irons.”

At those words, Knowles laid his head back on the pillow. He did not say more.

Ringo looked around anxiously. “Can I ask him something, Doctor?”

“Go ahead, Ringo,” Dr. Cole said.

“Why are you interested in my medallion, sir?”

“I know more than I want to know about that medallion.”

“But you couldn’t have known my father. You’ve been asleep for . . .”

Galan Knowles still seemed unable to do much but move his head. “That medallion you’ve got on, my boy, outdates any Irons family.”

“What do you mean, sir?”

“The first owners of that medallion lived thousands of years ago. They were the only race that could hold their own against the Nishka, a mighty people who were feared all over the known galaxy back before my time."

"Who were *they?*" Ringo asked.

"I was never able to completely understand it, but the Nishka were a people who had remarkable abilities. Nishka warriors rarely lost battles. Terror of them simply overwhelmed their opponents' minds, and armies fell before them."

"But how does Ringo's medallion fit into this?" Dr. Cole asked.

"The Nishka destroyed entire civilizations—including the brilliant Amesstorites. No one could stand against them except for the people of the man who wore that medallion—or one very much like it."

Both Ringo and Heck started barraging Knowles with questions, but Dr. Cole said loudly, "Enough! Out, you two! He must rest."

Soon the room was cleared except for Bronwen and the medical officer and the now still form of Galan Knowles.

Bronwen turned to Dr. Cole. "Is he unconscious, Temple?"

Dr. Cole was checking the space pilot's vital signs. "He's all right. He's just tired." Then she looked across Galan Knowles to the navigator. "What do you think he meant by what he said about the medallion, Bronwen?"

"I don't know, but I certainly wouldn't want to run into one of those Nishkas—or any of the people *they* couldn't defeat!"

"Nor would I!"

"I've never seen anything like that robot colony, Thrax," Captain Edge said. "And those Amesstorites.

The technology to make a warship that big—big enough to swallow a whole star cruiser—it's incredible!"

"Yes, it is, sir. And it appears the ship was intended primarily for defense after all. How do you think technology could have been so advanced five thousand years ago?"

"I don't think anyone knows. Amesstorite history is pretty well lost. But somehow they developed fantastic technology and medical skill—all of which has been retained through their robots."

The two men stood looking quietly out into space. Then Zeno added, "Computer research indicates that the mechanical anacondas were a major deterrent to humans' resettling Throsis. Along with the defensive warship, of course. I wonder if the race that had the intelligence to create such things is really completely gone now."

"In a way I hope so, but in a way I hope not. They were brilliant. Back five thousand years ago, Earth had no technology such as they had."

After another period of silence, the captain said, "I wonder what Galan Knowles will think of our civilization. It's so different from what his own must have been."

"I expect he'll have great difficulty. He's lost everything. He's like a man lost in a desert with nothing familiar."

The thought seemed to unnerve Edge. "I don't think I could take that," he murmured.

"With help he'll survive, and we'll all have to help him."

"We'll do that," Edge said. "We'll do all we can do, but only God can help with some things."

Thrax stared at his captain. It was probably the first positive thing he had ever heard Mark Edge say about God.

15

The Rejuvenator

After a while, Galan Knowles awoke from his deep sleep. As no one else seemed to be in sick bay, he decided to try getting up. He found that his legs were still shaky, but he leaned on beds as he hobbled about.

Suddenly he was stopped by an invisible force field. Perhaps this was a quarantine area, for beyond it lay a patient—a girl—who appeared to be very sick. He could tell that her breathing was labored.

At that moment the medical officer rushed through the door behind him. In her hand she carried a small mechanical device. Her face was shining.

"You are up and walking! God and your robot friend," she cried, "have given us the answer to treating Denebian dust syndrome!" The doctor switched off the quarantine force field and approached Mei-Lani Lao's bed.

Moments later the pink color of Mei-Lani's cheeks returned, her flesh returned to its normal healthy appearance, and the twinkle returned to her brown eyes.

"She's completely healed!" the doctor exclaimed. "What a remarkable electronic instrument! It will revolutionize Earth's medical science."

Mei-Lani Lao sat up, and a big smile creased her face from ear to ear.

Everyone on *Daystar* was aware that Galan Knowles, the man from the past, would be dropped off at Intergalactic Command. As the cruiser hurtled through space toward Earth, the Rangers decided to arrange a farewell party for him. They would use the rec hall, and the girls volunteered to do most of the decorating. Their biggest problem was keeping Heck Jordan away from the desserts.

A light atmosphere prevailed throughout the ship the evening of the celebration. The entire crew was invited, including the grunts. Tara Jaleel was reasonably pleasant. Even Ivan Petroski seemed to be happy. Jerusha had Contessa on a leash. She wanted no repetitions of the German shepherd's jumping on the captain.

Off in one corner, Dai and Raina were talking. They were somewhat alone for once, since the corner was cut off by a panel that separated it from the rest of the rec hall. Raina felt, for the first time in a long time, that Dai was paying complete attention to *her*.

He said, "Raina, we all know that my Aunt Bronwen loves everybody, but I think she has a special love for you."

"Really?"

"Oh yes. She talks about you a lot."

Raina leaned forward, then asked, "Dai, is there anyone *you* especially care for?"

"There certainly is!"

Raina crossed her fingers behind her back and held her breath. She desperately hoped to hear her own name from Dai's lips. "Who is it?" she asked.

"The whole *Daystar* crew is important to me," Dai said. He smiled gently. "They're like family, aren't they? I'd do anything I could for any of them, and I know that you would, too."

Disappointment washed through Raina. So that was that. She felt rather foolish. *Bronwen has told me more than once that I'm too young to be even think-*

ing about things like this. But she could not leave it alone. "Dai," she asked, "do you ever think of Sanara?"

Sanara. The beautiful princess who lived on the planet Cappella. The princess Dai had saved from the dangerous space locusts that were destroying her planet.

"Well, I suppose I liked her a lot, but that was all."

"You weren't in love with her?"

Dai stared at her. "I'm just not ready for that, Raina. Someday when I get older, I suppose I'll be thinking that God will send me someone to be my companion. But not now. Sanara was a fine girl, and her people are blessed to have her as their future leader, but she's not for me."

Raina had to be content with that. She stepped back and glanced across the room to where Ivan Petroski, Studs Cagney, and Zeno Thrax had gathered. "I wonder what they're talking about," she said.

Ivan, Studs, and Zeno leaned against a bulkhead and discussed the planet Throsis.

"I wonder what it was like," Zeno murmured, "for the Amesstorite people the first time they landed on that volcano?"

"They were probably scared senseless of both the volcano and the pit," Studs said. "*I* was."

Ivan Petroski nodded in agreement. "I never saw anything like those mechanical snakes. And to think that the things are still fully functional."

"They gave me the creeps," Studs said. "There must have been twenty of them all curled up in the bowels of that volcano."

In another corner, Heck and Ringo were quietly arguing. Heck wanted to show the data chips that he had stolen from the security computer.

"You can't do it, Heck. It'll cause all kinds of trouble."

"What trouble? Seeing that statue explode will be fun."

"You always say that something's fun," Ringo said, "until the trouble comes."

"Oh, there won't be any trouble. You worry too much. You need to take lessons from me on how to take life easy."

"You take life easy all right, and then you get into every pickle you can. I'm telling you, you'd better not show that video! Besides, Captain Edge won't let you."

Heck merely laughed. He was determined to make the video the highlight of the evening. He began to laugh to himself, thinking how funny it would be.

Ringo's eyes suddenly narrowed. "Let me see the data chips."

"Why?"

"Just for a minute."

"Why?" But Heck fished the stolen chips out of a pocket, anyway.

With one swoop of his hand, Ringo had them. He started across the rec hall straight toward Captain Edge, saying over his shoulder, "For your own welfare, Heck, I'm going to deposit these chips in a safe place."

"Wait!"

Heck stood with his mouth open.

When Dr. Temple Cole entered the rec hall, she was pushing Galan Knowles in a wheelchair. Mei-Lani was with them, walking, smiling, waving, and the very picture of good health.

Everyone stood and applauded.

Captain Edge waited until the applause had died down. Then he said, "We'd appreciate a little speech from you, Galan, if you feel up to it."

"I never was much of a speech maker," the space pilot protested quietly.

"Just a few words," Edge urged. "It doesn't have to be a long speech."

"Well, I will certainly speak my firm gratitude to all of you. God used you to find me—otherwise, I would yet be floating in space." Then he gestured toward Mei-Lani. "Just as He used my robot friend Primal One to save the life of this young lady. He always has people ready to accomplish those things that need to be done."

Galan Knowles actually spoke for some time. Finally he said, "Are there any questions?"

"Yes," the captain said. "I have one. You aren't yet on Earth, of course, but how do you find things today after five thousand years?"

The space pilot indicated the spacecraft with a wave of his hand. "Well, Captain Edge, the technology is remarkable, though I don't suppose that mankind itself will have changed particularly." Then he looked about at each one and said with a smile, "But if there are more people in the world like all of you, then I'm glad to be awake in it."

Moody Press, a ministry of the Moody Bible Institute,
is designed for education, evangelization, and edification.
If we may assist you in knowing more about Christ
and the Christian life, please write us without obligation:
Moody Press, c/o MLM, Chicago, Illinois 60610.